The Two-Bit Tango

a Nell Fury mystery

The Two-Bit Tango

a mystery
by Elizabeth Pincus

spinsters ink
minneapolis

First edition.
10-9-8-7-6-5-4-3-2

Spinsters Ink
P.O. Box 300170
Minneapolis, MN 55403

This is a work of fiction. Any similarity to persons living or dead is a coincidence.

Printed in the U.S.A. on acid-free paper.

Cover art by Miranda Lichtenstein.

The Spinsters desktop publishing system was made possible by a grant from the Horizons Foundation/Bay Area Career Women Fund and many individual donors.

Library of Congress Cataloging-in-Publication Data

Pincus, Elizabeth. 1957–
    The two-bit tango: a mystery / by Elizabeth
    Pincus. — 1st ed.
      p. cm.
    ISBN 0-933216-88-2 : $9.95
    I. Title.
PS3566.I517T87   1992
813'.54—dc20   92-17511
                                                CIP

For Jennie

Acknowledgements

I am grateful to the following people for advice, manuscript feedback and/or merciless needling: Shelli Ainsworth, Gloria Anzaldúa, Elizabeth Coffey, Julia Coley, Carole De-Santi, Susan Fleming, Mary Ingraham, Sue Marcoux, Erica Marcus, Joan Meyers, Vanessa Nemeth, Shaari Neretin, Stephanie Poggi, Jeannie Powell, Catharine Reid, Liddy Rich, Amy Scholder, Donna Tauscher, Patti Tauscher and Irene Zahava.

Special thanks to Sherry Thomas and the rest of the Spinsters staff for their smarts and good humor;

to Jennifer Mayer for her patience and loyalty through the years;

and to Jennie McKnight for helping out with a keen editorial eye, cold cash and hot guitar licks.

The Two-Bit Tango

a Nell Fury mystery

1

I was resting my elbows on the pitted bartop and making a dent in a fist-sized bag of mixed nuts when I saw her come in. She was lanky, a scared-looking brunette, but tough, too, like a pool room hustler with innocent eyes and a couple of tricks up her sleeve.

Uh-oh, I thought, licking a trace of salt from my upper lip. I'm a sucker for a woman with a secret.

I watched her sidle into the bar. She paused to give it the once-over, her wary glance washing past me with a tiny flicker of acknowledgement. It was enough. My pulse leaped around a bit and I took a long pull of St. Pauli Girl to steady my philandering heart. After all, I was supposed to be working.

She continued her appraisal. Then she moved—Miss America on the runway, tripped up by a bad case of nerves. I was dying. No one else seemed to notice. But then, I was the only other woman in the joint. I guess that's how she spotted me in the first place. Next time I'd wear my trenchcoat to avoid any confusion.

I swallowed some more beer while she conducted her business at the bar. She ordered a brandy and soda, left a lousy tip, and turned to catch my eye. I flashed a slow smile as she leaned onto the barstool beside me.

"Miss Fury?" she ventured.

I nodded. "Nell Fury."

"I'm Olive Jones."

Sure enough, it was the woman who'd phoned earlier. We shook hands. I gave it the old firm, no-nonsense clasp. She lingered a tad too long.

"What can I do for you?"

She released my hand and settled back on the stool, traces of fear flitting helter-skelter across her ashen face. Olive Jones had eyes the color of used motor oil, and I swear they were the size of saucers boring steadily into my own swamp-brown pools.

Something was up. Something major league.

"Nell...may I call you Nell?"

"Um-hm."

"My sister is missing. I—" More surreptitious glances. "Can we talk here?"

I perused the half-filled room. We were at the Mint, a homey spot on Market Street, halfway between the Civic Center and the Castro. The bar featured schmaltzy weekend sing–alongs with live piano accompaniment and burgers served out of the Hot 'N Hunky outlet next door. My kind of place.

I said: "We'll be fine, but let's move to a table." I nodded toward a sparsely furnished corner. Olive Jones headed that way while I bought another round. Then I joined her at one of those rickety linoleum numbers that really dresses up your average sub shop or bingo hall. This one was dotted with grimy rings from countless bar glasses. I waited while Olive drained half her brandy.

She finally remet my gaze, eyes somehow calmer.

"So Olive, why don't you start by telling me how you got my name and number."

"Yes, of course," she said. "I don't live here in San Francisco, I don't know anyone. At first I thought I could handle it alone but...now I don't know what to do. Yesterday I took a cab in from the airport. The driver was a lady, someone you know, Phoebe Grahame—"

Phoebe, a *lady*?

"—and she told me she knew a private detective. She said you were in the book." She hesitated a moment, sipped her drink. "You see, I need someone who's, ah, partial to women. Forgive me, I don't mean to be indiscreet."

"Go right ahead. Indiscretion's my middle name."

Her lips formed a wry twist. Way to charm 'em. She continued, "Yes, well, she also said you had a quick tongue."

"She should know." I grinned. Olive Jones was lovely when she blushed.

"Nell, I don't know many gay people. My sister is...that way...but I never met her new friends. We're from L.A. We're twins and we're very close. I still live in L.A., but she moved to San Francisco three years ago. Said she wanted to live here since she's a...a..."

"...lesbian?" I queried.

"Yes, yes. That's what she said. She tells me everything." Olive dropped her shoulders. "Or she used to."

"What's her name?"

"Catherine Jones. Cate. With a C."

"Go on."

"About two months ago she stopped writing. I called, but she was never home. Her roommate was hostile—I don't think she gave Cate my messages. Then several days ago I got a strange note from Cate that really frightened me. I kept calling but no one answered, so I came right away."

"Do you have the note?"

Olive reached into the folds of her coat, a voluminous, dark gray affair cut in that oversized get-thee-to-a-nunnery way. Stylish. She might be from Los Angeles, but she was no sun bunny. I wondered what Cate was like. As she drew out the slightly tattered envelope, I asked if the Jones twins were identical.

"Why yes, we are," she replied, husky-voiced. "Completely."

She handed me the envelope, a standard white business type, medium weight. Olive's name and address were printed squarely in blue felt-tip. I removed the single typed page, folded awkwardly in fourths. The typewriting on the note was faulty. It read:

Dear Olive,

   Sorry I haven't written. I got into trouble at the club. I didn't want to bother you but now I desperately need your help. Can you come to see me? Soon?! I'm at the same address.

The note was signed with a capital C, blue felt-tipped.

I looked up at Olive Jones. She was running her forefinger around the rim of her empty glass, caressing the moisture. She licked her finger slowly, then dropped her hand to her lap, nervous again before my scrutiny. I had a million questions.

I spoke, more gently than before.

"I assume you've tried to contact her since you arrived."

"Yes."

"No luck?"

"No."

"Called the cops?"

"No, I...it's only been a day and a half. I didn't think they'd listen to me."

I shrugged. She was probably right. It took either more time or more evidence of a crime to get the city's finest in on an adult missing persons case. "So you want to hire me to find her?" I asked.

"Yes. Please."

I pulled a business card from my jacket pocket. Phoebe had made them up for me, embossed gold lettering on pale pink bond: Nell Fury, Private Investigator — "I Like to Watch." I'd have to get new ones soon. The irony was lost on most of my clients.

I handed over the card. "Here's my office address. We can do the paperwork there tomorrow morning. But if you'd like, I'll get started now."

Olive nodded impassively. I went on: "I charge two hundred dollars a day, plus expenses. I'll need a six hundred dollar retainer up front."

She wordlessly reached for a slim alligator clutch. She slipped in my card, then withdrew six bills and tucked them without fanfare under my half-empty St. Pauli Girl. I hoped I looked nonchalant as I fingered their crispness, and shoved them into the well-worn pocket of my black jeans. I also pocketed Cate's note.

I took a sip of beer, too, to celebrate the transaction. It tasted so good that I polished it off, then suggested we go to Cate's apartment. I wanted to check it out. I told Olive my car was out of commission. I didn't mention how badly—it needed a new clutch and an engine overhaul. We decided to hoof it. She could fill me in on some Jones family background on the way.

My client was a little less skittish as we headed silently for the door. She even cracked a smile, revealing a couple of pinprick dimples. What a cutie. My newly adorned pocket crinkled as I passed by the Mint patrons, but I don't think they were raising their eyebrows at that.

2

When Olive Jones had called earlier that evening, I'd been typing a report and listening to John Lee Hooker on my clunky old tape deck. We'd agreed to meet at the Mint, one of my favorite rendezvous spots, so I quickly finished writing up my investigation into a mayonnaise heist that had operated out of an East Bay plant. It was an inside job. I had discovered a couple of warehouse workers making off with trunkloads of the stuff. I felt lousy about it; I had hoped to finger the management. Sometimes you don't know what you're getting into when you take on a case.

I had a few other reports to type up, too, and some detail work to complete on a tedious background investigation. But I was glad for Jones' call. It was Friday the thirteenth, after all, a good omen. And my caseload was a bit slack. I'd been in the business for four years—three for an agency, one on my own—and the clients seemed to come all at once, and then none for awhile. Kind of like the Muni buses on Mission Street.

Now I was walking up Market with Olive Jones. She had a few inches on me and I had to hustle to match her pace. Her neck was crooked downward, her coat flapping wildly around her scarecrow legs. She cut an odd but elegant figure in the gloomy dusk, like Anjelica Huston would look if she had a haircut.

We passed an oasis of brightness, the bustling parking lot of the 24-hour Safeway. Up ahead, a fog-shrouded sprinkle of lights rose from the residences scattered among the hills. I glanced covertly at Olive Jones. She was glancing covertly at me. Smooth, very smooth.

"Picturesque, eh?" I said.

She shrugged, averting her eyes. "I prefer the desert."

I scuffed my feet and tucked back an errant curl. Then I shivered in the mid-April twilight.

Cate's place was located just past the Castro, on a steep road ascending to Twin Peaks. Olive told me she was staying there; she didn't think Cate would mind. In fact, Cate had sent her a spare key some time before. As we headed for the apartment, I began prodding my client for details about her missing sister.

It seemed that Cate had moved a lot during her three years in San Francisco. She'd lived in the flat off 17th Street for seven months now, but Olive didn't know the roommate's name. They might be lovers, but she didn't know for sure. Cate was studying sculpture at the San Francisco Art Institute, and also took occasional jobs. She'd mentioned a dancing job recently. Olive figured she didn't mean polka or the two-step. Apparently the "club" Cate referred to in her note was the outfit that beefed up her already substantial income.

"Our parents are dead," Olive explained. "They were ...well-off." She told me she and Cate had no siblings, kids, husbands, cousins. No other living relatives, in fact. They were just a young set of identical twins splitting a cool couple of million.

I nodded. All kinds of motives suddenly danced around in my imagination. Money'll do that. I decided to hold my tongue. We arrived, panting slightly, at Cate's doorstep.

Olive whipped out her key. She shoved it in the Yale, twisted, and held open the door to a railroad-style Victorian flat. Stepping through, I felt like I'd seen this version of San Francisco apartment life hundreds of times before. It was all sleek hallways, Levelor shades, and muted rugs. I could see gleaming kitchen appliances at the end of a long corridor. Plants spilled from every sill and ceiling. I nearly choked on all the oxygen.

Olive went for coffee while I turned into a side bedroom in search of some clutter, some clues. It was spotless. A corner writing table sported no calendar, address book, business cards, or photographs. Only a streamlined mauve telephone graced the smooth white surface. I cupped the receiver and memorized the phone number printed neatly beneath the plastic strip. Then I opened the first of two drawers on the left, brushing aside some fern-like growth spurting from an earthen pot on the floor.

It contained stationery and envelopes, stamps in a roll, and a plastic domed paperweight with little white specks sludging about in blue-tinted water. I took a piece of the stationery and put it in my pocket, then lifted out the paperweight. It was labeled Harrah's, Lake Tahoe.

I shook it and snow cascaded down over tiny green simulated pines. I began to wonder if anyone really lived here or if we'd stumbled into a photo session of *House Beautiful.* Make that *House and Garden*, I thought, pushing aside another plant to open the second drawer.

This one held nothing but a matchbook from Club Femmes. Subtle.

Olive Jones entered with a cup of coffee for each of us. It smelled like the kind you get when you grind beans up fresh.

"Olive, does Cate know how to type?"

"Yeah, sure."

I stepped across the room to open a closet door. "Tell me if you recognize her clothes, her other things."

We traipsed about the whole flat, sipping coffee, finding few personal items. But Olive did spot clothes, furniture, books, and kitchenware belonging to her sister. The place still seemed remote and undomesticated, especially when Olive commented that her twin had never been so fastidious. Somebody'd done a calculated tidy-up. The bedroom with the Tahoe snowdome appeared to be Cate's, and a second bedroom seemed to house another tidy woman. But I found nothing to indicate what her name might be.

On impulse, I nabbed a threadbare cotton handkerchief with a brown and white checked border out of a wardrobe drawer and shoved it into my jacket. Good thing I had so many pockets.

Suspicion was knocking around in my head. I turned to brush another bit of plant matter from my shoulder, then realized that Olive Jones was trailing her fingertips across the nape of my neck.

I jumped. She jumped. We each took a few more hops backwards. If we'd had a rope, we could've gotten in some decent exercise.

Tears were welling up in Olive's Pennzoil eyes. "I...I've never done this, Nell. I just thought maybe..." Her voice caught. "Maybe you'd spend the night."

I regained my woman-of-the-world composure. My attraction had suddenly evaporated. All I could smell was trouble.

"You've been reading too much Raymond Chandler," I said. "I only sleep with clients if they're *ex*-clients. And then only if they're lesbians."

The tears came down. I put an arm around her, gingerly, and led her back to the kitchen. I didn't know if she was crying because I said no, because her sister was missing, or because she was all alone in a strange city. Maybe she was weeping over this crummy world where even being rich can't buy you everything you want. I was a little short on sympathy.

I said goodbye. Olive Jones poured herself another cup of joe. No wonder she was so jittery. I left her that way, huddled over the polished butcher block table. Sniffling, she agreed to call me at home if Cate or the roommate showed up anytime that night. Otherwise, she would meet me at my office tomorrow morning at nine.

On my way out, I checked the mailboxes by Cate's front door. No identifying labels, no junk mail, nothing but a band of gooey adhesive running across the top of the black metal box. Someone had ripped off a name tag, quite recently.

I decided to stop for a nightcap before going home. I backtracked down 17th and headed for the Castro. There was a lot of foot traffic on a Friday night. Nearing Collingwood, I could hear the racket from Francine's and a couple of men's bars. I smiled. I was born and bred in Cleveland, but San Francisco felt like my real home town.

Francine's, a hole-in-the-wall corner bar, had wide windows opening onto the streets along two sides. Tonight the place was sardined with wall-to-wall dykes. It made me feel very sane. I could see Lou bouncing around behind the bar as if she were built like a jockey instead of a shotputter. I squeezed forward and peeked over the counter to see if she was wearing a pair of those new sneakers with air pumps. That would explain it.

Nope. Cordovan penny loafers, probably about a size twelve.

"Hey, Nell. What's doin'?" She wiggled an eyebrow at me through her Gloria Steinem aviator glasses.

I love that about Lou. She's always about two decades behind the times.

"Get this, Lou," I yelled above the din. "I just turned down a proposition." That swiveled a few heads.

She shot me a quizzical look. She was busily stirring a sickly blue concoction with one hand and popping open a Corona with the other. "What happened?" she asked.

"I don't know." I paused. "She was straight."

Lou laughed. "Since when are you so fussy?"

Good point. I asked for a Jameson's, neat. She brought it over and I sipped on it slowly, wondering why I felt so uneasy about Olive Jones. I was worried that Cate had been kidnapped; a ransom note could appear any day. Or maybe *Cate* was the bad guy here, and had lured Olive up north with an eye on swindling away the family dough. Hell, I'd been reading too much Chandler, too. Cate and her mystery roommate were probably having a romantic *pas de deux* at a Russian River resort. Some missing person.

Lou was leaning forward, arms crossed on the bar in front of me. "Nellie, I heard you cracked that case over at the AIDS Treatment Clearing House."

"It cracked me, was more like it." I told her how I'd ferreted out some corruption among the honchos at ATCH. It had happened a couple of weeks before, but my left arm was still recovering from a knife gash and a separated shoulder I'd received during a brawl with the director of the organization.

"Anyway," I said, "I uncovered a murder and a lot of dirty politics."

Lou chuckled. "You're so modest."

We talked a little about the upcoming San Francisco AIDS conference and the international boycott brewing because of the U.S.'s exclusionary immigration policies. Land of the free. Ha.

"Anything new cookin'?" Lou asked.

"Oh, you know me, babe, 'The Eye That Never Sleeps.'"

We both laughed. I was always making cracks about that Pinkerton slogan.

Thirsty customers were pressing up to the bar. Lou said: "Gotta go. The women, they're always clamoring for me."

"I bet they are, Louie."

I left her a short stack of bills and headed into the chill night. I zigzagged home to my apartment on Ramona Avenue, a short walk east, across Dolores Street. Stepping over my threshold, I wearily scooped up my mail and shut the door. One thing about traipsing all over this congested little town on foot: you never had to worry about parking.

3

I started making calls the next morning at nine-thirty when Olive Jones had failed to show up for our appointment. I tried her at Cate's apartment—no answer. I checked the phone number in my criss cross directory. Sure enough, it was listed as the number for the apartment off 17th Street, only it was under the name G. Finer. Aha. I also checked for Catherines, Cates or C. Joneses in the regular Bay Area telephone books. Lots of Catherines and Cs. I could start trying them later if my other leads ran dry.

I called the San Francisco Art Institute. A recorded message told me to call back during business hours. Saturday mornings *are* my business hours, I thought grumpily. I found Club Femmes in the trusty White Pages. Someone answered, but he hung up on me when I asked if Cate Jones was around. I tried Cate's apartment again. One, two, three strikes you're out. I started thinking about how many Joneses there are in the world. It got me reminiscing about my favorite childhood TV show, *Alias Smith and Jones*. Hmmm.

I let my fingers do some more walking, this time through the Los Angeles phone book. Olive Jones had told me she lived in her family's house in Pacific Palisades, a ritzy enclave snuggled up in the canyons northwest of Santa Monica. No Olives or Catherines listed in Pacific Palisades, but maybe the number was still in their parents' name. I jotted down the numbers for all nineteen Joneses I found listed in Pacific Palisades. Just in case.

By now it was almost ten-thirty. I was frustrated, blurry-eyed, hungry, and worried. I decided to hightail it back to Cate's. Maybe Olive was only sleeping late, but I remembered my uneasy thoughts of the night before. I left a note for Olive on the outer door, in the event she turned up after all.

My office was located on Tennessee Street, near Mariposa, in a decaying neighborhood of industrial buildings, mangled railroad tracks, and long-abandoned hash houses. I probably would've been banished from here if the new ballpark proposed for this area had been approved. It hadn't, so I was secure for now. My office was in my friend Mary's warehouse. She painted here at night, and let me put in a phone and desk to do business in the daytime. I had intended to get a real office in a well-trafficked neighborhood as soon as I could afford it, but I was getting attached to this spacious hovel by the bay.

The fog was sitting heavily across the brackish waters of China Basin as I unlocked my Schwinn from a rusty pipe at the edge of my building. My ailing VW Rabbit was stalled in front of the warehouse loading dock, collecting gull droppings. I didn't know whether to fix it, junk it, or give it to Mary for one of her mixed-media installation pieces. In the meantime, the Schwinn was my ticket to ride. Phoebe had painted the old ten-speed in orange and black tiger stripes. I always felt kind of jazzy rolling down the street.

I cut west and north to get to a flattish route that would take me on a straight shot all the way over to the Castro. I detoured briefly to pick up a bran muffin at the Port Deli. It must have weighed five pounds. Hope it worked.

By the time I'd tackled the uphill portion of 17th Street, I was sweating underneath my black jeans and standard issue white T. A piece of paper was fluttering from a tack on Cate's front door. I took a closer look. It was a note to me, from Olive—gee, we were practically pen pals by now.

"Nell," she had written across the top, her letters slanting just a hair to the left. She said:

> I'm out looking for Cate. I'm sorry, I was too anxious to wait. Can we do the paperwork later? Will you meet me at The Box tonight, on Divisadero? It's Cate's Saturday night hangout—God, I hope she's there. See you after 10:00 p.m.
>
> Olive Jones

Shit. I had the cash money, but no contract, and that always made me nervous. Besides, if she wanted to run around playing Nancy Drew, why did she hire me in the first place? Maybe she was just gun-shy about seeing me after last night. Nell Fury, heartbreaker.

I rang the doorbell for good measure. No one appeared to be inside; nothing seemed amiss. Time to hop back on the two-wheeled speedster. The downhill cruise from lower Twin Peaks to Market Street dried off all my sweat, even as dollops of sun started poking out from between the clouds. I was on my way to the Club Femmes to see if it lived up to its name.

There wasn't a *femme* in sight as I entered a side door to the Turk Street dance emporium. The front doors were locked. That was okay by me, considering that the handles were painted to resemble a couple of breasts adorned with sparkling fuchsia falsies. A woman's bikinied crotch was painted down below. It looked like you'd split her right in two if you opened the doors.

I'd spotted the side entrance when I peered down a narrow alley to the left of the building. The rectangular steel door was propped open with a cement block, maybe to air out the joint. Through the hazy darkness, I could make out a cavernous room painted a dull matte black. A few track lights revealed a long runway across a far wall, with bar supplies behind it. Except for the runway, the place reminded me of a music club in Minneapolis, the 7th Street Entry, where I'd worked the door during my freshman year of college. Another uneventful episode in my life, though I did get to see The Contractions a few times—and Prince, before he hit the big time.

I was traversing the sticky floor when a gravelly voice rose up from a corner behind the runway. "You wanna audition?"

I halted. Gravel Voice abandoned whatever he was doing and lumbered across the room in my direction. He measured about 5' 2", his legs a couple of tree trunks in dirt-smeared khakis. When he got closer, I noticed his eyebrows hung onto his face like twitchy caterpillars clinging to a tree limb. His skin had a greenish tinge.

"No," I said.

"I didn't think so. You're kinda chunky." He leered. "Nice jugs, though."

"Well, as long as we're trading impressions, you've got one ugly puss," I said, striding off toward an open doorway I'd noticed across the room.

"Fuck you! Hey! Where ya goin'..." He lunged after me.

I turned to brace myself. No way I'd let him touch me. Just then, a figure appeared in the open doorway. He told Gravel Voice to stop. Only he called him Melvin.

"What's happening here, Miss?" This new guy was as pretty as Melvin was hideous. Tall drink of water, silvery hair, the kind of jaw that set the standard for comic book heroes everywhere.

Melvin interrupted. "This broad thinks she's real cute."

"No I don't. But I think I've got a good personality."

The tall fellow tried to suppress a smile. Maybe he was smarter than he looked. I didn't know if that was a good thing or not. He told Melvin to get back to work, then asked me what I wanted. When I requested a little privacy, he ushered me through the inner door. We were in some kind of office.

"Sorry about Melvin. He's, uh...protective."

"You really need that kind of muscle around here?"

He shrugged. "Rough part of town." He nodded me into a mustard-colored Naugahyde chair, his eyes doing a vertical up-and-down as he watched me sit. I swear, some men must have a genetic condition that makes their eyeballs rove and their necks crane whenever women are around.

I asked him who he was. Godfrey Bellinski, owner-manager of Club Femmes.

"I'm Nell Fury," I said. "I'm looking for Cate Jones. I think she works here."

I was watching his eyes closely, but I couldn't tell if they flickered at the name. He just smiled, as placid as a summer afternoon. "Sure, she works here, but not on weekends. Come back next week. Monday, Wednesday, or Thursday night."

"Her sister thinks she's missing. Was she at work this past week?"

Bellinski frowned. "Who did you say you were?"

"Detective Nell Fury."

He shrugged. Probably thought I was a cop. "Yeah, she was here."

"Tell me, Mr. Bellinski, did you know Cate Jones is a woman of, ah, independent means? Why would she—" I laughed lightly, implying no offense intended. "Why would she come to work here?"

Bellinski laughed too. Ha ha ha. There went those eyeballs again. "You see, Miss Fury, some of the ladies find the dancing...erotically pleasing. And we treat them well. Some would even call my club feminist." It came out like a hiss.

He added, "The ladies can even join a union."

"How progressive of you." If he knew I was being sarcastic, he didn't let on. I'd heard there were a couple of porn places in town—Lusty Lady, the infamous Mitchell Brothers—that attracted feminist and lesbian dancers and were, in fact, good to them. Whether I believed that or not, I didn't get the impression that Club Femmes qualified as pro-woman. Or pro-worker.

"Well, I guess I'll check back next week, if necessary." I stood up. "Oh, one more thing. Have you got an employee here, last name of Finer?"

This time Bellinski paused too long. "No. No. But who knows—the ladies don't always give us their real names. What can you do?"

I darted out of there quickly, to avoid having to shake his hand. My friend Melvin was nowhere in sight as I retraced my steps. A group of young women had congregated near the side door, chatting. The club must be opening soon.

Only a couple of them bothered to look over at me as I walked out. A woman with a tangle of shoulder-length braids and a perfect milk chocolate complexion flashed a smile my way. A stunning redhead—not chestnut-red like me, but that pale, almost transparent orangy-red—stared at me coldly. I raised a hand in a sisterhood-is-powerful wave, and scurried out into the sunshine.

4

Rounding the corner onto Taylor, I ducked into a Vietnamese restaurant and walked briskly toward the back, like I knew where I was headed. I found a bathroom with no trouble, and ordered spring rolls to go on my way out.

The Tenderloin was a happening place on a Saturday. I knew it had gotten even more crowded since the Loma Prieta earthquake—more buildings condemned, more people without homes. The Marina District had received a lot of publicity after the big quake, but renters in the low-income neighborhoods were the ones really hurting. Besides, affordable apartments and single-room occupancy hotels were already in trouble from the condos and luxury hotels closing in on all sides.

I glanced up at the Hilton highrise, towering over the Tenderloin from its plot a few blocks north on O'Farrell Street. It was like Boston's Combat Zone or New York's Times Square: embattled neighborhoods of hookers, junkies, queers, and immigrants trying to fend off the property-hungry developers.

I fetched the Schwinn and decided on one more stop before going home to recoup. It was a killer ride from the

Tenderloin to the far side of Russian Hill. I made it, though, stopping only once to walk the steepest blocks of Leavenworth Street. The way I figured, I was earning every nickel of my 600 dollars.

The San Francisco Art Institute was housed in a funky old building overlooking Fisherman's Wharf. The elite school was known for churning out cutting-edge, if somewhat pampered, artists. The first time I'd visited, to see some wacked-out experimental films, I'd expected an appropriately mod structure. Instead, you walk through a graying stucco entranceway into a Spanish-style interior courtyard with a molding fish pond in the center. Or maybe it was supposed to be a fountain. In any case, I'd never seen anything in it but algae and cigarette butts.

A modern addition had apparently been added on to the school at some point. An airy cafe with an open patio looked out toward Coit Tower. The studios were situated in well-lit rooms that staircased down a back slope. A fair number of artists were lounging or working amidst the cheerful clutter. Nobody paid me much attention.

I mosied around looking for the sculpture studios and finally found them. A twenty-ish man was feverishly hacking away at a small chunk of marble. I was sure the original stone had been prettier than the mangled lump he was now creating. What a pity.

He turned when he heard me walking his way. He sported a crew cut, diamond stud earring, Grateful Dead T-shirt, and pink madras slacks. Flicking off his Guns 'N Roses cassette, he threw a scowl in my direction.

"Good afternoon," I said. "Have you seen Cate Jones? I was hoping to find her today."

His scowl deepened. "Naw."

"Do you know her?"

"Yeah. I mean, we're not *friends* or anything. I know who she is."

I wondered if he hated lesbians, or just all women. I went on, "Well, I run a small summer arts colony up in Mendocino. Cate won a grant from us, but she hasn't responded yet. If she doesn't accept by Monday, we'll have to give the grant to the next candidate. I just need to talk to her."

He blinked at me. "You don't look like no arts administrator."

"Yeah, well, you don't look like a Dead Head either." Sometimes it's hard to maintain a pretext in the face of such a jerk. I forced a smile. "Look, I guess she's not here today. Maybe you know where the student files are kept? Her application said she's in L.A. on weekends. Maybe I could get that address and reach her there."

Not too convincing; I wasn't even sure what I was looking for. But a glance at the files would give me her Social Security number if nothing else.

Mr. Dead Head was sufficiently duped, but he wasn't very helpful. He told me the school's administrative offices were all locked on the weekends—and the custodians wouldn't let me in without permission. The files were probably confidential anyway, he added as an afterthought. Smart boy.

I wasn't adverse to breaking into places, but there were too many people around to do it right then. I was about to leave, when he mumbled that I should check the sculpture department's mailing list. It was posted around the corner on a bulletin board.

I left him to his masterpiece and went to peruse the list. Cate Jones, temporary address: the now-familiar lower Twin Peaks apartment. Permanent address: 437 Toyopa Drive, Pacific Palisades. Bingo.

5

I was snacking on Fritos and a tin of smoked oysters when Phoebe Grahame returned my call at seven-thirty that night. I'd left a message with the dispatcher at Barbary Coast Cab for her to get in touch when she got off work. I'd had time to shower, put on clean trousers with a fresh white T-shirt, and watch the evening news. Former mayor Dianne Feinstein was re-emerging as a serious contender in California electoral politics. She was getting lots of media time these days for her innovative platform: pro-choice *and* pro-death penalty.

"She's so damn calculating!" I fumed to Phoebe when I picked up the phone.

"Who? That woman you met last month at the recycling center?"

"No no no. Feinstein! She thinks she'll get the abortion rights people *and* the death penalty types in her pocket—as if everyone's so single-issue focused they'll put up with that. Besides, her ties to big business are as strong as ever. And she still masquerades as a liberal! It's disgusting."

"I don't know, Nell. Makes sense to me. I mean, her opponents would argue a murder is a murder."

"Hmmpphhh!" I could hear Phoebe chuckling. I knew she agreed with me; she loved it when I got on a political jag. It made her feel less crazy.

"So what's the squid?" she asked.

I smiled into the phone. I hadn't seen Phoebe in a few days and I missed her. She was my best friend, my favorite ex-lover, and the comeliest taxi driver in the City That Knows How. The first time we had sex was in the back seat of her cab, parked on a deserted stretch of the Embarcadero. It was one of those ridiculously starry evenings. Phoebe left the radio tuned to a nonstop blues program and afterwards we shared a bottle of cheap red wine and stayed up all night. In retrospect, the whole thing was incredibly hokey, but I still couldn't hear her voice without feeling wistful.

I asked: "Wanna go to The Box with me tonight?"

"Whoa—are you getting trendy?"

"Nah." I laughed. Phoebe knew I preferred Francine's and Amelia's, old-school lesbian hangouts where the butches looked like butches and even the femmes wore pants. Both bars were in financial trouble, I'd heard, and it made me apprehensive. The Box—like other party spots that were only open on certain nights—was a relative newcomer. Lipstick and miniskirts were more common than not. But it was also supposed to be more mixed, race-wise and gender-wise, and it offered more adventurous music. Time to check it out.

I explained I was meeting my new client there, the one she'd referred to me. Phoebe asked about the case. I gave her an abbreviated rundown. I was circumspect about the details, even with Phoebe, though she could be a big help sometimes. She was one of those people who knew all the inside dirt on local politicians and personalitites. Cabbies are good that way.

She agreed to pick me up in a couple of hours. We rang off and I fixed myself a tomato sandwich to finish my supper. Harriet always ate them in *Harriet the Spy*. That's why I liked tomato sandwiches, but also because you could load them up with lots of mayonnaise. Too bad they didn't give me a few bonus jars for solving the great mayo caper.

At 9:45 p.m. I was waiting on my Ramona Avenue stoop, admiring the cerulean sky. My daughter Pinky had taught me the word "cerulean." As an aspiring poet, she was handy with obscurities like that. Pinky—whose name had been Madeline before she opted for a more, um, lively nickname—was fourteen years old and just out of her punk phase. Now she was drawn to black turtlenecks and the legacy of the beat generation. She wasn't a bad poet herself, if you liked that kind of thing.

Pinky lived in London with her other mom, my first ex-lover Caroline Zule. Caroline and I had raised Pinky together until we split up. Now we shared custody. It worked out okay. Pinky seemed to enjoy her quasi-dual citizenship, especially now that she was older. But I always missed her when she wasn't with me. She'd be here soon, though, for the summer, no doubt eager to haunt the North Beach hangouts of the beat poets.

Phoebe rolled up in her ancient Plymouth Duster and disturbed my reverie. I slid in beside her and kissed her dewy cheek. She looked like a brunette version of Jean Seberg in *Breathless*.

"Hey sweetheart," she said, "you really dressed up!" She was referring to my string tie with the rhinestone cowboy boot clasp. I'd thrown it on at the last minute.

"Yeah." I grinned. "That's me, Nell Fury, fashion-plate."

We set off for the Western Addition, just a short drive across Market and past the Duboce Triangle. The night felt oddly still as we headed for The Box's entrance. I thought I saw Olive Jones slip through in front of a gaggle of young women who looked like they'd stepped out of a John Waters movie. Phoebe paid our covers, and I squinted into the smoky interior.

There she was, executing that familiar nervous shuffle along a near wall. I was irritated with my client, but thought I'd play it cool and assess where we were at. I'd even brought along a contract—hopefully she'd agree to sign it in some quiet corner. It'd be just like high school, cutting deals in the bathroom.

"Olive!" I called out to her.

She kept walking. "Hey." I picked up my step. "Hey Olive..."

She turned, jostling a couple of guys who were right on her footsteps. She peered around them and scanned the room, looking right past me. I frowned, and raised my hand in that windshield-wiper move you do to get people to notice you.

"Olive?" I felt an acidy jolt in my gut. The woman finally met my eye, brows dipping with annoyance. She sighed.

"I'm Cate Jones. Olive's sister."

I gawked. Except for the outfit, they were identical indeed, right down to the screwball attractiveness. I couldn't believe it; after all, Olive and I had been up-close-and-personal for a few moments there. I stepped closer. Cate was wearing a tight pair of Sixties-style hiphuggers and a black velvet headband—certainly different from Olive's fashion statement of the night before. But their features were indistinguishable.

She stretched her lips at me. "You're Nell, right? Olive said you might show up. She told me to tell you she's sorry. She worries too much sometimes. Anyway, she found me!" A squeak escaped from her throat. "I mean, I was never lost. I guess I should stay in better touch with her—"

"Where is she?"

"Who? Olive?"

"Yes. Olive." I was feeling very rattled.

"Oh. She went home. She caught a flight back to L.A. this afternoon." Cate Jones groped a side pocket of her hiphuggers. I couldn't believe anything would fit in there.

She handed me an envelope. "Olive wanted to offer you a little more, for your trouble."

There must have been a score of C-notes in there. I gaped at her again. "What the hell?"

Cate Jones was getting sick of me. She tightened her jaw. "Like I said, she's sorry. Now I've gotta go." She set off for the door.

I called after her, "But you just got here!"

"No. You must be mistaken. Bye." She sprinted.

"Wait..." I took a few steps, then stopped, rooted to the spot. What was going on? I considered following her, then thought better of it. She just told me it was all a false alarm. So I was done. No missing person—no client. Case closed.

What I had, though, was a pawful of cold cash that I didn't deserve. I shrugged, looking around for Phoebe.

I found her on a barstool across the room, a glass of red wine in one hand and a Bud in the other. The Bud was for me. I told her what had happened.

"...so I guess I should double-check with Olive. Make sure she's okay. Then drop it."

Phoebe nodded. "What about that note, you know, the one that Cate sent about being in trouble?"

"She must have worked it out. Whatever it was."

I remembered a case in which a couple had hired me to find their son. I found him. Turned out he was gay, and had been routinely abused by his parents. I told the parents I had failed. Maybe Cate Jones was another family member who preferred staying lost.

Phoebe was poking me. "Do you know how to get in touch with Olive?" she asked.

"I've got her address. And a bunch of possible phone numbers." I paused. "Do you think I should return the money?"

"Nope."

"I don't know..."

"Nellie. She doesn't need it—you do. Get your car fixed. Or trade it in for a better one."

"I don't need a car!"

"Who ever heard of a private eye without a car?"

I thought really hard. "Jessica Fletcher!"

Phoebe groaned. The bartender accepted my Ben Franklin and returned with another house red and a Bud. I shoved the change into the envelope, and put the whole wad in my pocket. Phoebe and I had fun that night, lingering right on up until last call.

6

My alarm woke me at eight o'clock. I would've put on my outfit from last night, only it smelled too smoky. I found a pair of black jeans under my bed and pulled them on, along with a semi-clean T. I laced up my oxfords, grabbed a jacket, and was out the door.

The It's Tops Coffee Shop around the corner was almost empty. I ordered coffee and an English muffin, and settled back with the Sunday paper. The Cubs were off to a mediocre start. Par for the course. But they had a dynamite new pitcher named Harkey, a stable of solid hitters, and some leftover confidence from last season.

I'd been a Cubbies fan since I spent a summer in Chicago at age twenty. That was thirteen years ago, when Caroline and I were together and Pinky was an infant. Another lifetime. Maybe I still read the box scores and checked TV listings for the rare Cubs broadcast in order to remember those days in Wrigleyville.

The English muffin was stale, so I loaded it with butter and honey. Umm, delicious. I dawdled some more over the Pink Section. Then I paid my tab to a hard-faced lad at the register and sauntered onto Market Street. I was feeling flush, so I caught a cab to my office. Too early to make phone calls, but there was other work I could polish off.

A few hours later I had typed two reports, paid a couple of bills, and jotted some notes on the outstanding background check. I'd have to finish that one on a weekday. There were a few query letters in yesterday's mail, which I skimmed hopefully. I wrote to one of the correspondents and referred her to an agency that does high-tech investigations. I'm more of a low-tech sort, myself.

Another request I flat out denied—no way I'd work for the Traditional Values Coalition. How had they gotten my name, anyway? I filed the other letters for tomorrow. Once I talked to Olive Jones, I'd feel more free to contact new clients.

I also took a few minutes to compare Cate's note to the piece of stationery I'd lifted from the apartment. They were of similar heft and could have come from the same stock, but that didn't tell me much. Either Cate or her roommate could have written the note, or anybody's aunt could have picked up a box of the paper down at Walgreen's. It still didn't make sense that the note was so poorly typed. Or that it was folded in quarters. People who knew how to type usually did the standard two-fold method of inserting a letter in an envelope. Big deal. If Cate was shook up, maybe she just got sloppy.

I re-locked the note in my bottom desk drawer. A forensics expert could trace the paper's watermark or check it for prints if it turned out to be necessary. The handkerchief I'd taken from the apartment was also stashed in the same drawer.

I glanced at my list of the nineteen phone numbers for Joneses in Pacific Palisades. Hmmm. It would simplify my task if I knew any phone company employees in L.A. I didn't, but maybe Tad did. Tad Greenblatt, my friend from the Continent West Detective Agency, had a ten year head start on me in developing contacts. I placed a call. Tad wasn't in, so I left a message for him to call me ASAP.

Meanwhile, I might as well start dialing. I got a few wrong numbers, a couple of answering machines, some endless rings, and one hostile hang-up. No Olive, or anyone who knew Olive or Cate Jones. Shit. I had talked myself into not worrying about Olive, but there were still so many oddities to the whole situation. I kept remembering Olive's lovely, stricken face. Tad called while I was contemplating things.

"Hiya Nell."

"Tad-ulah!" Tad was my favorite man. In fact, he got me started in the business. When I moved back to the States after five years in London, I came to San Francisco and took a job as a deckhand on the Red & White Fleet, ferrying tourists back and forth across the Bay. Tad was called in by our union to investigate the shady dealings of one of the company vice presidents. Tad and I had a conversation one day during the run to Alcatraz, and we really hit it off. I was tantalized by his occupation.

He helped me get hired at Continent West. It was one of those two-bit operations that took on novice employees and just about any sleazy client who came in the door. Tad loved it there and stayed on for the camaraderie and legitimacy an agency can provide. I liked it, too, but decided to leave Continent West after the requisite three years to get my solo license. Working for myself suited me much better. I'd been bouncing around from city to city and job to job for more than a decade, and I'd finally found a calling I could stick with for a while.

I told Tad what I needed and gave him Olive's address. Even that hadn't helped me get anywhere with the regular information operator. Tad said he knew an inside source and would get back to me that day. I hung up and plopped into my magenta leather easy chair, the only other piece of furniture in the warehouse besides my desk and a few ratty stools. I might as well wait until Tad called back with a telephone number. Phoebe was picking me up soon, anyway. I'd agreed to join her for a day at the races.

Golden Gate Fields was crawling with cigar-chomping old-timers when we strolled in at ten minutes before post time. The East Bay racetrack was newish and had a clean-cut feel, a far cry from its dusty counterpart on the peninsula, Bay Meadows. With a bare-boned interior, decaying grandstand, and mottled old viewing ring, Bay Meadows exuded an aura of sin and decadence. By contrast, Golden Gate Fields felt about as racy as Six Flags Over Texas. I didn't care—I loved the atmosphere. And Phoebe loved to play the ponies.

She went off toward the pari-mutuel windows, *Racing Form* clutched tightly under her arm. I went searching for the snack bar. We reunited a few races later. Phoebe was up about thirty clams. I was down the cost of a Polish sausage, a pack of peanuts, and a draft. Phoebe was making notations on a program and eavesdropping on a guy in a fedora who was raving about some filly named Frisky Business.

"I don't know, Nellie..." Phoebe scratched her head. I looked over her shoulder. Her jottings looked like hieroglyphics to me, but I noticed a horse named Gwen's Folly running in the Fourth against Frisky Business. I might have to put a few dollars on Gwen's Folly. Her odds were at 15-1, but my mother's name had been Gwen. She'd always faced tough odds, too.

I said to Phoebe: "Let's go check 'em out."

We walked over to the viewing ring. Gwen's Folly was schlepping around the circle with as much energy as Rosa Mota at the end of a marathon. Frisky Business, on the other hand, was stepping tall, a proud toss in her bay-colored mane. I'd go with Gwen's Folly anyway; her jockey was a woman wearing lavender silks.

I followed Phoebe to the betting windows. We were standing in line when she suddenly elbowed me.

"Hey!" I protested. She almost made me drop my beer.

"Isn't that Jed Flack?" she whispered, pointing to a fifty-ish white guy standing one line over in a stone-washed denim jacket.

It sure was. Flack was a city supervisor, a five-year veteran on the contentious board that oversaw San Francisco city politics. He came down on the progressive side of things, most of the time. Like about a third of the board, he was up for reelection, and scrambling for endorsements from various local politicians and organizations.

"What's he doing here?" Phoebe asked, still whispering.

"Same thing you are, sweetheart." I pointed to the program rolled up, baton-like, in his hand.

"I've been hearing rumors about Flack. One of the gay Democratic clubs is tracing his political background. You know how he says he's been pro-gay and pro-tenant all along? Somebody who knew him years ago in Nevada says that's a sham."

"He's from Nevada?"

"Yeah. I think he moved here in the Sixties to go to grad school."

The lines were inching forward. Flack took a step. I noticed a flashy woman at his side, dressed all in black with a polka-dotted band around her bolero hat. A shock of short red hair poked out from the sides. I blinked. It was the woman I'd seen at Club Femmes.

They placed their bets, then walked away in the direction of the outdoor bleachers. I quickly put six dollars on Gwen's Folly to win, place, or show—I'm such a chicken—and four dollars on Wait For Me, another long shot, to win. Last minute impulse. Phoebe was dropping a bundle on Frisky Business. I scurried off to find Flack and Polka Dots. "I'll be in the winner's circle!" I yelled to Phoebe.

I approached Polka Dots with my arm outstretched. Just call me Miss Friendly. "Hello there!" I said. "I didn't catch your name yesterday—"

She jerked and started to scowl, then stopped herself. I wondered if she was about to put on an act for her quasi-famous companion. She thrust her hand into her jacket pocket and fixed me with a bland stare. Flack, meanwhile, was looking off at the tote board, but I could tell he was listening very carefully.

She said, "Are you following me?"

That was a laugh. I mean, I follow people all the time, but I try to do it discreetly. "No. Listen, sorry to bother you, I was looking for my friend Cate yesterday, Cate Jones. I thought you might know her..." I let it trail off.

"I can't help you," Polka Dots snapped. "And we're busy right now." She nodded at the horses and riders getting situated in the starting gates. "And besides, I don't want to talk to you!"

Well, there you have it. I shrugged at her and walked away. The gun sounded. I watched the fillies pound their way around the dusty track. Wait For Me finished first, Gwen's Folly second, and Frisky Business straggled in a dismal seventh. Phoebe would kill me. I smiled.

Later that evening I was sitting at the Roxie Theatre, a movie house in the Mission District, waiting for the show to start. I was chomping my way through a box of Milk Duds. There had been a message from Rae on my answering machine when I got home from the track. She was the woman I'd met recently at the Mission recycling center. Our tortuously slow romance had so far included a lot of after dinner drinks, hand holding, and tenuous kisses. I had hoped to coax her to the movies tonight, but she wasn't home when I called. I hummed a riff from Carly Simon's "Anticipation" and popped another Dud.

There had also been a message from Tad. He'd left Olive's number in Los Angeles, culled from his phone company source. I called it a bunch of times—there was no answer for several hours, just the droning message of a phone machine. It sounded like Olive, but I couldn't be sure.

I went back to Cate's apartment, too. Nobody home. After fuming a bit, I decided to go to L.A. the following day, just to ease my mind. I wanted to talk to Olive Jones in person and make sure I could finally resolve this sorry case. Or non-case. Phoebe said she'd lend me her car.

The Roxie was having an Agnes Varda retrospective. I'd come to see *Vagabond* for, umm, about the third time. Something about the waifish Sandrine Bonnaire wandering back roads in hopeless desolation just pierced my heart. The movie opens with the discovery of a young woman's body, then moves through a bunch of weird characters and murky motives. Hey! It was just like a French feminist version of *Twin Peaks*. No—*Twin Peaks* was like an *anti*-feminist version of *Vagabond*. I'd have to mention this theory to my semiotician friend at San Francisco State. She loved that kind of nonsense.

7

Phoebe's car didn't have a tape deck. It didn't have FM either, just a tinny AM radio that crackled in and out of focus as I sped south on the Bayshore Freeway. It was good enough for Phoebe—she loved Top 40 tunes—but it drove me nuts. I snapped off the radio and started belting out a medley of Nell Fury's favorite hits. "...gotta stop sobbin', uh huh, yeah! YEAH!" Chrissie Hynde had mellowed a bit with the marriage routine, but I still loved her. After all, we were both Ohioans.

I cut off 101 just north of Salinas for a quick detour to Castroville. I slowed the car when I saw the Giant Artichoke looming ahead. A huge, green, reinforced concrete artichoke rose up against the cloudless sky, marking the site of a fast-food restaurant and fruit stand. I paid for an order of fried artichoke hearts and wandered over to the adjoining souvenir outlet. A couple of fellows in pastel All American Boy T-shirts were trying on Giant Artichoke aprons, laughing uproariously. Sometimes you just had to love California.

I picked out an artichoke keychain for Pinky. She'd ODed on Elvis trinkets during our trip to Memphis last year. This new item ought to please her.

After choosing some ripe peaches for the road, I pointed the car toward Salinas and met back up with 101 going south. This route was a little longer than Highway 5, but much more scenic. After all, I wasn't in that much of a hurry. I figured I'd get to L.A. right before rush hour and find Olive Jones. Then take in some nightlife, perhaps, and return home to the grind tomorrow.

By following the Phoebe Grahame method of selective lawbreaking, I pulled into the Los Angeles area about an hour and a half ahead of schedule. But I'd forgotten it was *always* rush hour in L.A. I cut south on 405, then west on the Santa Monica Freeway, which dumped me onto the Pacific Coast Highway.

I had one of those Thomas road bibles flipped open on the seat beside me and I used it to find the best exit for Pacific Palisades. I headed into an area of impossibly steep bluffs with dramatic foliage and partially-hidden rustic homes. Olive's street wasn't hard to find. It was parallel to one of the main roads that intersected with Sunset Boulevard. I turned onto Toyopa and rolled to a stop in front of a Fifties era bungalow that had been modernized with tasteful metal sculptures dotting the front lawn and Japanese-style topiary leading off around a side patio.

I set my emergency brake. It was a good fifteen degrees warmer here than it had been up north. I tossed my jacket in the back seat and strode up to the front door. The bell was encased in a miniature pagoda ornament. When I rang it, I heard a melodic chime echo within the house.

"She's out of town, dearie!"

I turned to watch a tiny woman traversing the lawn with a standard poodle in tow. It was the hugest dog I'd ever seen, a chocolate brown puff ball that towered over her, drooling on her helmet of silver pincurls. She looked a bit like a turtle, all hunched up with a shrively neck and a wide, protruding mouth. She "tskked!" at the dog as it lifted a leg on one of the *objets d'art*.

"Hello," she said. "Are you a friend of Olive's?"

"No, actually, I knew her mother better. I was in town and thought I'd stop in and see how the gals were doing."

"Ohhhh." She shook her head. "Well, Cate's gone and moved to Frisco. Some time ago, it was. And Olive, she's away visiting her right now. I'm happy about that—they were always so sweet together." The head wagged again. "What's your name?"

"Marcia. Marcia Rhodes," I said, sticking out my hand.

She pumped it. "Well, isn't it a small world! I'm Martha! Marcia, Martha...ha ha!"

"Do you know when Olive is due back?"

"No. She wasn't real exact about it. I'm watching over her puppy—"

"That's a puppy?" I pointed at the brown monster, now loping in circles, twisting its leash around Martha's legs.

"Ha ha ha! No, this is Doris—she's mine. Olive's little mongrel is inside." That cracked her up all over again. "So anyway," she continued, pausing to wipe her nose on a tissue, "I can't tell you exactly when Olive will get back. She's been out of sorts lately, not to blame her. She ever tell you about that boyfriend of hers?"

"No."

"Humpphhh! He was a piece of work. Nice-looking, but a real mean fellow. He dumped her, alright, then up and moved to Frisco." Her turtle mouth spread even wider. "Folks around the neighborhood, they thought maybe he and Cate had something going on up there, but I knew better. Cate didn't take much to the fellows..." She got embarrassed all of a sudden.

I smiled reassuringly. "Yes, I know."

Martha tied Doris to a porch railing, then stepped up, nabbed a key from atop the door frame, and fitted it in the lock.

I said: "Martha, mind if I come in and use the bathroom? I've been on the road for hours."

"Of course not, dear. Come on." I followed behind her as she pushed the buttons to deactivate one of those numbered security alarm systems. I strained to see the numbers—I hoped I'd gotten the right sequence. The house smelled like lilacs, with a tiny hint of dog piss. A cute little mutt came yapping up the corridor and skidded into Martha. "Ha ha ha! Well, go on, I'll be in the kitchen feeding her."

I cut to the right as Martha headed in the opposite direction. Where the hell was Olive Jones? Maybe after losing her boyfriend and being rejected by me, she'd fled to the arms of some other mystery lover. She could be anywhere, actually, and I still didn't know if it was my business any longer.

I cased the house as best I could with Martha puttering around in the kitchen. I satisfied myself that there was no one here, and no signs of disruption or foul play. I also satisfied myself in the bathroom—I really did need one after two A & Ws in the final stretch of my drive. Then I spotted a photo of Cate and Olive, arms draped rakishly across each other's shoulders, on the narrow sill. It went into my back pocket, delicate silver frame and all.

I strolled back to the kitchen, taking in the faux Japanese decor and the casual moneyed comfort of Olive's home.

"Thanks. I guess I'll be off."

"Oh, there you are. Okay. I'll tell Olive you stopped by."

"Thank you, Martha. Say—" I paused. "Where has Olive been working lately?"

She squinted at me. "She doesn't work, dear."

"Oh, yes, well. I'm not sure she knows how to reach me. Will you give her this—ask her to give me a call?"

I handed her a business card from my pack of tricks. This one said, "Marcia Rhodes, Consultant," with my home phone number only. I smiled at Martha. "Feel free to call me yourself if you're ever in San Francisco."

She glanced at the card and tittered. "Oh! You're from Frisco, too! Isn't it a small world?"

I nodded agreement. But honestly, the world felt very large just then.

8

I found a motor inn in Santa Monica, a one-story stucco affair just a few blocks from the ocean. I paid the bill in cash and signed in as Marcia Rhodes. A sleepy-eyed kid in a maroon terry cloth robe looked up from *People's Court* just long enough to hand me a room key.

It was getting on toward six o'clock when I stepped back outside. There was a pungent smell of eucalyptus in the air and a salty breeze taking the edge off the afternoon heat. I dodged traffic to get to a take-out salad joint across the street from the motel. I heaped a paper tray with sprouts and avocado. When in Rome. Maybe I'd even take a stroll on the beach at sunset.

I carted the salad—blue cheese dressing on the side—back to my room. Flicking on the TV, I lounged on the bed, avoiding the lumps and a suspicious mushroom-shaped stain near the center of the chintzy coverlet. I found a channel with a sports update. The Cubs had swept a three-game series with the Mets. I messed around with the flicker some more before settling in for a local newscast. I kicked off my shoes and dug into the plate of greens.

I snapped alert. A bouffant-headed Sally Field lookalike was reading a story about murder in San Francisco.

"...Melvin Held was notorious in Los Angeles for his alleged connection to convicted arsonist Joe Lockenwood. No proof was ever found, however, to link Held to the series of Hollywood fires that shook up residents and business owners in 1985, and Held had been out of the public eye ever since Lockenwood's trial. The discovery of Held's body this morning outside a nightclub in San Francisco's Tenderloin District..."

Damn. How many Melvins could there be hanging around the Tenderloin? Just then, the station flashed a photo of Held. It was the furry-eyebrowed lug from Club Femmes, alright, apparently before years of gin-guzzling had done a number on his jowls.

Sally was yammering on. There was renewed speculation that Held was involved in criminal activities in the Bay Area—perhaps his murder an act of revenge by hostile associates. The police were offering no comment. Big surprise.

I picked up the phone. Tad must have been screening calls because he chimed in when I identified myself.

"Hiya Nell."

"Hey, Tad, what do you know about that murder in the Tenderloin?"

"Which one?"

"Guy named Held. L.A. mob connections, it sounds like."

"Oh. That's a crock of shit. He was just a no-good thug."

"How do you know?"

"Trust me, Nellie. What broadcast are you watching? The media's just looking to blow it up—generate some headlines, you know."

"I'm in L.A. What're they saying up there?"

"What are you doing in L.A.?"

"Could you answer my question first, please?"

"Yeah yeah." Tad told me that Melvin Held had been found that morning in the alley off Turk Street with his head smashed in. Probably by a cement block. His boss had called it in, guy name of... Tad couldn't remember. I asked if it was

Godfrey Bellinski. Yup, that's him, runs a porn place where Held worked.

"Are you mixed up in this?" Tad asked.

I hedged. Then told him about my encounter with Held and Bellinski just two days before. "...and Tad, you know that woman I was trying to reach? Olive Jones? I came to L.A. to find her. She hasn't come home."

Tad was silent. My brain was buzzing double-time. "Come see me when you get back to San Francisco," Tad finally said. "We'll talk about it."

"Yeah."

If I left Los Angeles right now, I'd have to fight to keep my eyes open, and I'd still arrive home after midnight. I decided to nap for awhile and hit the road at 2 a.m. I pulled the shades but had trouble falling asleep, so I went out for that walk on the beach after all. The water's edge felt coated with a slimy residue and there were more rusted bottle caps to be found than seashells. I gave it up and headed back to the motel, muck squishing around in my soiled oxfords. I suppose I managed a few hours of sleep before my travel alarm clanged at 1:45 a.m.

I skipped the shower and slunk out to the Duster. This time it was Highway 5 north, no detours.

9

There was a plainclothes dick waiting for me when I turned onto Ramona Avenue the next morning at eight-fifteen. He was a dead giveaway in his powder blue undercover vehicle, *Chronicle* folded open to the comics and styrofoam cup fogging up his windshield. There were a few other cups decorating the dash—maybe he'd been waiting for me all night. Good. We'd be in about the same mood.

I pretended to ignore him. I was digging for my apartment key when I heard his car door slam. Geez, did he have to wake up the neighbors?

"Your name Fury?"

I pivoted. He was about my height, a whip-thin man in a sharkskin sport coat with a thatch of biscuit-colored hair. He was wearing photogray glasses so I couldn't see his eyes. His hands were on his hips, index fingers pointed at his crotch. I don't know why guys do that—I'd know where to look if I cared to.

"Who's asking?" I said.

"Cute. S.F.P.D., homicide." He flipped a badge, much too fast to get a look at. I decided not to push it.

45

"You have a name?"

"Inspector Little."

"Well, Mr. Little—" Boy, my mood was really picking up. "—I'm Nell Fury. How can I help you?"

"We're taking a ride. We need to have a conversation. Downtown."

"May I ask what this is about?"

His hands left his hips. He joined them together, cracking back all the knuckles. "Uh huh. It's about your connection with the Club Femmes." He rhymed it with "gems," drawing out the final "s."

"Look, Inspector, I'm not going to be able to help you. Besides, I'm really beat. How about I shower, freshen up, come see you at the station later on?"

Little sneered. "Lady, we're all beat here, okay? You were overheard arguing with Melvin Held, recently deceased. You're coming *now*."

I could have refused, asked for a lawyer, trumpeted all my civil rights. But I decided to get it over with. Maybe I'd even find out something useful.

Little took me to the cop house over on Ellis. I spent a few hours with him and his cronies, sipping warmed-over sewer sludge and answering the same queries over and over. Amazing how many different ways they could frame the same question. I invoked client privilege. Told them only that I'd been on a case that had dead-ended at Club Femmes. In fact, I said, the case was closed.

I didn't get much in return, except they told me it was Godfrey Bellinski who had named me. That was odd; why would he point the finger my way? To deflect suspicion away from Held's ties to the L.A. arsonist? Or maybe Bellinski was pissed when he found out I was private heat, not a cop. The boys in blue seemed to be grasping at straws. I got the impression they had very little crime scene evidence to go on.

Little said he'd be in touch. I didn't doubt it. I hoofed it home, with a side trip to El Toro on Valencia to pick up a super deluxe chicken burrito. My stomach gnawed and the dull pain in my left shoulder kicked back into a steady throb. The burrito took care of my stomach, but my arm was killing me. I lingered in a steamy shower to try and ease the pain.

I listened to my phone machine messages as I dried down with my favorite Holiday Inn towel. Phoebe had called—she was worried since she heard about Held's murder. No hurry on returning the Duster, she said. Tad wanted to talk to me, too, but I already knew that. My brother Harry had called. So had Lydia Luchetti, a journalist who was a constant thorn in my side, but also an important contact. Then my heart flipped when I heard Rae's mellifluous voice. Another missed connection.

I made a mental note to return all the calls that night. Meanwhile, I dialed the number of an acquaintance who'd spent a lot of years on the state beat for the *San Jose Mercury News*.

She told me she remembered when the Hollywood fires had made headlines—August of 1985. That's all I needed. I drove down Market to the main branch of the public library. By the time I emerged from the microfilm room an hour and a half later, I'd discovered one interesting fact in the *Los Angeles Times*: one of the establishments torched that summer was an L.A. porno palace called the Club Femmes.

I parked the Duster around the corner from Cate's apartment. If I couldn't find Cate or Olive, maybe I could get a lead on the alleged roommate, G. Finer. No one answered the doorbell, nothing new. I carried my clipboard to the flat next door. No one there, either. When I rang the bell at the Victorian on the other side of Cate's, someone finally appeared. This neighbor was a light-skinned Black man in a lime green Brooks Brothers shirt and a pair of square tortoiseshell glasses. He looked at me blankly.

"Hi there," I said. "I've been trying to contact the people next door for a week. Do you know if they're away?"

"No." He studied me more closely. "Why?"

I lifted my shoulders in a big exaggerated heave. "Census." I flashed a phony credential, taking a lesson in speed from Inspector Little. "They're holding up my paperwork for the neighborhood. You know, I don't get paid until I turn in all the forms."

He smiled. "Must be a bear of a job."

"Yeah... Maybe you could tell me how many people live there, their names and stuff?"

He looked puzzled. "Don't you need signatures or something?"

"No." Actually, I had no idea how the census worked.

He peered at me some more. "You look kind of familiar..."

Shit. He must have seen me lurking around Cate's. I quickly fibbed: "Maybe you saw me last year at Gay Pride. I was in the front row of Dykes on Bikes."

"Yeah?" He grinned. "I was in Gays for Patsy."

We beamed at each other for a moment, basking in that we-are-family glow. "So anyway," I said, "about your neighbors—"

"Yeah, what the hell. Two women live there, Gillian and...I guess I haven't met the new one. Just seen her around." He chuckled. "Gillian's popular with the girls."

I raised an eyebrow.

"I guess it's that luminous halo of hair. She's no angel, though." He chuckled some more.

I swallowed a gasp. Cate's roommate and lover, Gillian Finer—the same woman I'd seen at the track with Jed Flack? And at Club Femmes?

I pretended to scribble something on my clipboard. "Do you know if the women work outside the home?"

"Like I said, I don't know about the new roommate. But Gillian does, sure. Downtown at a club. Matter of fact, she works at that place that's been in the news—"

"Club Femmes?"

"Yeah, that's it. Weird shit, huh?"

"You said it. Well—" I shook his hand vigorously. "Thanks a million. I'll look for you at Pride. Patsy Cline lives!"

I was out of there before he had a chance to think twice about our screwy conversation. Hustling toward the Duster, I noticed a figure on Cate's front steps, eyes pressed to a window, trying to see into the apartment's entranceway. A tumble of braids fell onto the shoulders of her jeans jacket. I called out "Hello!" and trotted up the stairs.

"Oh!" she said, looking confused as she turned and saw me. It was the other woman from Club Femmes, the one who'd smiled at me. Maybe there was something to Martha's "It's a small world" theory after all.

"Aren't you—" she began nervously. "I mean, weren't you applying for a job the other day?"

"Not exactly." I decided to trust her. "I've been trying to find Cate Jones."

"Me too! God, I'm so worried."

I asked her if she wanted to talk about it. She said sure, and we settled on Francine's—as good a place as any. I gave her a ride down the hill and told her I wasn't a friend of Cate's, but a private eye. That widened her eyes.

"My name's Nell Fury." I handed her a business card.

"I'm Mallory Valdez."

"That's a lovely name."

"Yeah." She grimaced. "I liked it better before Exxon made it a household word."

I didn't get it at first. She prodded me. "You know, the tanker?"

"Ohhhh." I liked this woman. She drank a Bloody Mary and I stuck with Bud, and we passed a somber happy hour sharing our concerns about Cate Jones and the Club Femmes.

10

"...so we got to talking. Between acts and stuff. Cate was practically inseparable from Gillian; really dependent on her. Like Gillian had brainwashed her or something. But Cate seemed kind of lonely anyway. Know what I mean?"

"Sure." Mallory Valdez was telling me about her friendship with Cate. And how she started worrying when Cate didn't show up for work again last night. I asked, "How long has she been missing work?"

"Ummm...I guess about a week. Gillian says she's sick, but I don't know if I believe her. I mean, she's just acting so nonchalant—"

"Gillian?"

"Yeah, Gillian. It's like, the rest of us have been all upset since they found Held's body. But Gillian—she's as cool as all get out."

"Is that unusual?"

"I suppose not. But you'd think she'd be more anxious with everything going on down there."

I sipped my Bud. "What do you mean? At the club?"

Valdez nodded. "There's this other weird thing, Nell. Bellinski—you met him, right?—Bellinski's been pulling some of us aside. Asking if we want to do more than dance. 'Expand our repertoire,' he says. He's kind of vague about it, just hints at more money. Know what? I think he wants to start pimping." She paused. "I gotta get out of there."

I asked her how long she'd been working for Godfrey Bellinski. She told me about a year. She also said Gillian brought Cate in about six months ago and helped her get hired. According to Valdez, Gillian Finer went back even further. She couldn't tell me much about the history of Club Femmes, though, except she'd heard somewhere that Bellinski bought the place within the last five years. She didn't know anything about an affiliated club in Los Angeles.

"Ever seen Jed Flack at Club Femmes?" I asked.

Valdez tilted her head.

"The city supervisor—"

"Oh, right. No. I don't think so..." She shrugged.

I told her Bellinski had said the dancers could join a union. She snorted. "I can't believe he'd take credit for *that*. Have you heard of COYOTE?"

I nodded. "Call Off Your Old Tired Ethics."

"Right," Valdez said. "It's organized by women—sex workers. Some of us go to meetings, but it's not like Bellinski has anything to do with it. Patronizing creep!"

Francine's was starting to swell with the after-work crowd. I settled our check, leaving an extra big tip for Lou. I walked Mallory Valdez over to the underground Muni stop at Castro and Market. Before she took off, I mentioned seeing Cate at The Box on Saturday night. That baffled her.

"Cate was supposed to be too sick to get out of bed," Valdez explained.

We said goodbye, with a promise to keep each other posted. I retrieved the car and headed for home. The sky had turned gray since I last noticed it. I was exhausted.

Straggling up the stairs to my apartment, I wondered what to do with all the information jumbling around in my head. I felt inextricably involved. I still had the wad of cash, and now the cops were on my case. And I kept remembering Olive's big wet eyes, boring into mine with that skittish mixture of need and wariness. Damn. Where was she?

Reaching the top of the stairs, I thumbed absently through the day's mail—nothing from Pinky. She was my only regular correspondent, and lots of days had gone by. Ah well.

Inside, I kicked off my shoes and padded into the kitchen to look for sustenance. I snagged a pack of Licorice Whips from the stash in the cupboard and sat on the stool near the telephone. I dialed Phoebe first. Listening to the rings, I ripped open the cellophane and bit into a hunk of black licorice.

"Hello?"

I said: "Phoebe Grahame. My own true love."

"Nell! That's '*mine* own true love.'" I could hear the relief in her voice, but she quickly tried to squelch it. Phoebe knew I hated for people to worry about me. "We missed *Fury* again. It was at the Castro last night."

"Rats." I'd been wanting to see that old Fritz Lang movie for years. "What else have I missed?"

"Well, I went back to Golden Gate Fields yesterday and recouped some of my losses." Phoebe waited a second. "And I suppose you heard about Melvin Held?"

"Yup." I told her briefly about my quick jaunt to L.A. "So now I'm missing two twins instead of one. What do you think?"

"I think Cate Jones discovered something fishy going on at Club Femmes."

"Hmmm. Get this, Phoebe—turns out that woman we saw with Jed Flack, remember?"

"Yeah?"

"That's Cate's lover. Her name's Gillian Finer."

Phoebe caught her breath. "No shit..."

"Heard anything more about Flack, by the way?"

"No. Want me to ask around?"

"That'd be great. And Phoebe?"

"Yeah?"

"Mind if I keep the car another night?"

She laughed. "Nope. Just park it on Ramona and I'll pick it up tomorrow afternoon."

"Thanks."

I remembered all my phone messages from earlier in the day. There were a couple of new ones, too, including a second message from the ever-earnest Lydia Luchetti. Sighing, I decided to blow most of them off for now. Tad I would contact tomorrow. But Rae?

I took a deep breath and punched her number. No answer. Phew. That done, I opted for a nap. I set my alarm for midnight and fell immediately into a solid sleep.

11

I'd left a light on by mistake. When I jerked awake, the glare burned into my eyeballs and I reached over to snap it off. A streetlight outside my wide front window let in a nice muted glow— that I could handle. I lay back for a minute to take in the comfortable muddle of my one-room flat under the eaves. God, I was sleepy. I forced myself up and reheated some coffee from earlier in the day.

My clothes were wrinkled from my brief nap, but then, my clothes were always wrinkled. I yanked on a baggy sweater and contemplated my oxfords. They were still all mucked up from the Santa Monica beach. I found an alternative pair of shoes tucked in the far recesses of my closet. They were a gift from Phoebe—soft brown ankle-high leather boots with small silver buckles along the sides. I thought they were a bit precious myself, but I was showered with compliments the one time I'd worn them. Shows you what I know from taste.

I tugged them on. I also donned a clunky pair of black glasses with clear lenses, and squished my hair into a battered green felt hat. Probably wasn't necessary, but a little subterfuge couldn't hurt.

A parking ticket was littering the Duster's windshield when I stepped outside a few minutes later. I was parked too close to an intersection or something. I jammed it in my back pocket and rolled off toward Market Street. The radio was spitting out a late night talk show about Feinstein and the elections. I listened for awhile, feeling cranky. There was a fair amount of traffic on the roads; it picked up even more as I neared the Tenderloin.

According to Mallory Valdez, Club Femmes dancers worked in staggered shifts, so they got off at different hours depending on when they started. She had told me Gillian was scheduled to dance that night until 1 a.m. The employees usually left by the side door, the one leading into the alley where Melvin Held had been killed. A few parking places at the end of the alley were reserved for Club Femmes workers; first come, first served.

I pulled up to a fire hydrant on Turk Street. I could see the alleyway from here, and felt inconspicuous enough. Plenty of people were hanging around down here this time of night, some of them in or nearby their cars. A blast of caustic music was coming from a top floor window across the way. It was 12:40 a.m. by my watch. I waited.

If Cate emerged with Gillian Finer, I planned to confront them. If Gillian was alone, which I figured was more likely, I'd simply follow her. If Gillian was with someone else, well, I'd have to see who it was. Flexibility—that's what they stress in my *How to Become a Successful Private Eye* manual. I was game.

1:15 a.m. came and went. A clump of women spilled out at twenty past the hour, but no Finer. I was starting to get edgy when she walked out ten minutes later. Apparently she'd changed clothes. Through the semi-darkness, I could make her out in jeans and a plain dark overcoat. Her hair practically glowed in the shimmering light of a nearby neon sign. She didn't even look back as she strode to a four-door compact parked down the alley.

I let her get a block ahead before juicing up the Duster and falling behind her into the Turk Street traffic.

Surveillance is a game which works a lot better with two people in the car. It works better still with multiple cars leapfrogging around to keep the shadow varied. I didn't have the luxury, though, and besides, I liked the challenge of working a tail. Gillian Finer was on a straight shot so far, driving west on Turk. She eased into the left lane of the one-way street and took a left at Hyde Street. I jogged over, too. She crossed over Market and headed south of the slot, signaling a left turn at the Bryant Street on-ramp. I followed behind onto the freeway.

It looked like Finer was heading east across the San Francisco-Oakland Bay Bridge. I stayed reasonably close as we rounded a curve, though I felt exposed in the relatively sparse traffic up here. When I saw her enter the lower deck of the bridge, I settled in about three cars back, fighting the tiny jolt of panic that arose at the thought of the Bay Bridge. I'd never felt the same about crossing it since a section collapsed in the '89 earthquake. I laughed a little at the arbitrariness of my fears.

We were over in a few minutes. Finer stayed in the center lanes, and I sped up closer to avoid losing her to any of the options she could take now that we were in Oakland. She merged onto 24 east. I let more space build up again as we cut through the darkness of the increasingly empty roadway. I took a few deep breaths and tried to relax my grip on the steering wheel. I realized I was tensing up all over.

Gillian Finer kept heading east, and I followed her through the Caldecott Tunnel. We were in the suburbs now, a stretch of wealthy bedroom communities nestled among the hills of Contra Costa County. Suddenly, she signaled a right turn and I was trailing her slowly down the off-ramp toward the town of Orinda. I felt really conspicuous now, but if she noticed anything she wasn't letting on.

An ornate deco sign for the Orinda movie theater loomed up over a tiny commercial strip just off the highway. The only time I'd been to Orinda was to go to the theater. It was during a period of community struggle over the fate of the movie house, one of those old-fashioned palaces with plush velvet seats and flowery *bas relief* decorations lining the interior walls. I remembered the movie was lousy, but I'd felt good about supporting the establishment.

Finer passed downtown Orinda and turned off Moraga Way just a short while later. I cut my lights and proceeded to snake behind her up a winding road. She made two more turns before crunching to a halt in a circular stone driveway behind a gleaming white Camaro. I saw her enter through the front, then I cruised past until I'd rounded another bend. I trotted back on foot.

There were lights on here and there in the spacious, tree-shaded homes, but no people in sight and no sounds of activity. I crept alongside the house that Finer had entered until I could see the front door. I made a note of the street address which was visible in the arc of a porch light. No noises emanated from within.

So did Gillian Finer have a house out here? Another lover? Maybe she and Cate were living at this place—that would explain the abandoned feel of the apartment they were supposed to share in the city. I thought about breaking in, but decided it would make more sense to come back when I knew Finer was away. I also debated waiting out the night and seeing where Finer was headed the next day. But there were too many other things I could be doing. Sleeping, for one.

I trudged back to the Duster and pointed it down the hill. Ten minutes later I was speeding west on 24, retracing my route to San Francisco. The parking place I'd deserted on Ramona Avenue was still vacant so I slid back in. Lightning wouldn't strike twice. I collapsed on my bed without removing my clothes; sat up again when I had trouble falling asleep. I flicked on the light and groped around on the floor among a pile of library books. I found the one I'd started and dug into the fourth chapter of *G is for Gumshoe*. Kinsey, you son of a gun.

12

I needed to follow up on a few things before Phoebe fetched the car, so I pulled myself out of bed at 9 a.m. Fifteen minutes later, I left the apartment. Wouldn't you know—a parking ticket, this time for street cleaning. It wasn't the Duster's fault, but I kicked it anyway. I stopped at It's Tops long enough to pay for a cup of coffee, then sipped it gingerly as I rolled over to the freeway entrance at South Van Ness. Repeating last night's drive, I crossed the Bay Bridge, but proceeded past Orinda and on to the city of Concord.

I parked at a meter and dutifully dropped in a coin. It was toasty in the East Bay, far from the gusts of Pacific air that keep the tip of the San Francisco peninsula perpetually chilled. I left my sweater in the car and approached the municipal courthouse for Contra Costa County.

These things differ from region to region, but you can usually find information on property deeds in the vicinity of the civil courts. Negotiating bureaucratic mazes was one of my least favorite things about private detecting, but this time I lucked out with a no-nonsense clerk and a well-organized system for recording who owned property in various parts of the county. In just a few minutes, I located information on the address I'd visited last night. The place was owned by Godfrey Bellinski.

Good lord. So Gillian Finer was tight with Bellinski. And she was also friendly with Jed Flack. If A equals B, and A equals C, does B equal C? It made sense to me, but then those equations never included variables like, what if B were double-crossing A? Or C slipping a mickey to B? And where did variable D, Cate Jones, fit into the whole mess?

The only motive I could attach to the disappearance of Cate and her sister was the oldest one in the book: money. But as far as I knew there'd been no ransom request as yet. Maybe love was hovering around in the picture somewhere, too. Or perhaps the Jones twins *were* connected with the arson case in L.A. and the death of Melvin Held.

I gave a high sign to the clerk, who fiddled with her horn rims before tucking back into her copy of *PC World*. I stepped outside, blinking against the mid-morning sun. A rusty pay phone was squatting like a weary sentry at the foot of the courthouse stairs. I thought for about one second of calling the San Francisco cops. Instead, I pushed in a quarter and dialed Tad at his office at the Continent West Detective Agency. He agreed to meet me back in the city for lunch at the Mission Rock.

I detoured past Bellinski's house on my way back, contemplating the best time to check out the inside of the premises. Clearly, not right now. Bellinski and Gillain Finer were reposing on the front porch, sharing coffee from a silver urn and what looked like a plate of Danish pastry. How cozy. I half expected the Beave to come running up the walk with a big "Hi!" for Ward and June.

I hurried by, noting another vehicle in the drive behind Gillian's little compact. The Camaro was gone; the new car was a hunky copper sedan, some kind of Mercury. The angle was all wrong to read the license plate. Bellinski and Finer looked up from their newspapers as I passed, but I was zipping too fast for them to make me. I wondered if they were putting on a show of normalcy for their suburban neighbors—just a couple of mellow Californians enjoying each other's company and the majesty of a perfect spring day.

Tad Greenblatt used to be called The Refrigerator until a certain pro football player usurped the affectionate nickname. Tad wouldn't answer to it anymore, but you get the idea how he's built. Add a mangled nose that curved down his face like a fish hook and a set of hard gunmetal eyes, and you had one intimidating fellow. It didn't work on me, though. Tad reminded me more of a B-movie character actor than a real live arm-breaker. But then, he was usually on my side.

I found him polishing off his first cheeseburger at a table overlooking the water at Pier 52. He ordered another and I followed suit, along with a large root beer, hold the ice. I liked my drinks warm-ish. Tad checked out my footwear as I slid onto the bench across from him.

"Aren't you a picture," he said, dumping catsup over the last of his charred fries.

"Met your match, huh?" I could tell Tad liked the swanky brown boots I was wearing again. He was always looking for ways to improve himself sartorially—he had some crazy notion he'd be a more effective investigator if he dressed like a professional. A professional what, I wondered, used car salesman? His latest ensemble consisted of a buttery yellow tie that matched his yellow acrylic socks, a gray and blue seersucker suit, coordinated deep gray loafers made of crushed patent leather, and a turquoise shirt that brought out the blue in the jacket. Sharp, I guess, if you lived in Miami.

"I'm glad you called, Nellie," Tad said. "I was talking to some of the boys yesterday. Your name came up."

"Hmmm." The waiter brought my root beer. I peeled the paper off a straw and dunked it in.

"Yeah," he continued, "they wonder what you were doing at that porn joint. I'm sure I don't need to tell you this, but the owner, what's his name—"

"Bellinski."

"Right. Bellinski's no doubt bought himself some protection at the S.F.P.D. I don't know from who, but they're not crazy about you coming in, maybe messing up the, ah, arrangements."

I shrugged. "Aw, I'm small potatoes."

"Not any more you're not. Since you broke that thing over at that AIDS outfit, they think you merit a little observation. In fact, they think you could be trouble. With a capital T."

I was almost flattered. "Well, I hope you disabused them of that notion."

Tad smirked. "What do you think? I didn't say a damn thing. Made me wonder, though. A two-bit creep like Held gets his bell rung, permanently, and the cops are all bent out of shape. You and I know there's a missing person angle, but they don't. She's still missing, right?"

"Yup." I explained that both twins were, in fact, unaccounted for.

"Huh. Well. The whole thing got me curious, so I made some inquiries."

Our lunches arrived just then; my first, his second. I added mayo and a river of catsup and made a stab at wrapping my mouth around the entire concoction. I dribbled some grease down the front of my white shirt. Heck, it needed washing anyway. Tad was grinning at me when I looked up.

"So," I prodded, "you were telling me about your inquiries."

"Right. I'm working a case for this pipsqueak assistant D.A. down in Orange County. Tracking a missing witness. This guy's a clown, but he knows people in L.A." I smiled— Tad nurtured his sources indiscriminately. "So I threw the names Bellinski and Held at him. He tells me Held was publicly linked with the guy who started those Hollywood fires—Joe Lockenwood. But there wasn't enough proof to convict him and Lockenwood wouldn't flip. But here's the part that *didn't* make the papers. The L.A.P.D. also thought *Bellinski* was in on the arson plan. They could never pin it on him, though, and they've kept it hush-hush in case they needed some ammunition against him in the future. It looks like it was an insurance scam gone awry—"

I interrupted. "So you know one of the buildings that burned in L.A. was called Club Femmes?"

"Yeah." Tad looked surprised, then went on. "Bellinski's place. So he came up north to start over, but his insurance money got tied up in the courts. So how'd he have the capital to open a new nightclub?"

I slurped some root beer. "Did Held have any money?"

Tad shook his head.

"Well," I continued, "maybe Lockenwood's cohorts helped out." Did that make any sense? If Bellinski kept his mouth shut, perhaps they rewarded him with a little start-up fund.

Tad was nodding. "Yeah, could be. Lockenwood'll be out soon—maybe looking to do business again with Bellinski."

I knew from reading all those back issues of the *Los Angeles Times* that no one had died in the Hollywood fires. Lockenwood cut a deal and got off easy. So maybe he had some reason to want Held out of the way now. But what about the Joneses?

I listened to the choppy bay waters slapping rhythmically against the side of the pier. A dead fish smell wafted across the Mission Rock patio, adding a gamy layer to the odors of sweat and fried hamburgers. At a table behind me, a cadre of angry young men was making a lot noise about something. I glanced over. Matching James Dean T-shirts, combat boots, crew cuts with long sideburns. Hmm. It could be a hardcore rock band, a bunch of skinhead punks, or a gay activist group—hard to tell them apart these days. I smiled when I noticed the pink triangle tattoo on one of the guy's biceps.

Tad pushed away his plate and fired up a Chesterfield. I leaned in for a whiff of second-hand smoke. The zealotry of the anti-smoking movement really got on my nerves sometimes. Almost made me want to pick up the habit again. I chewed on a dill spear instead and gave Tad an update on Olive and Cate.

He scrutinized the picture of them I'd brought along. He didn't say anything about it, just handed it back. We talked a little more and agreed that the house in Orinda was due for a little B and E.

"Be careful," Tad said.

I guffawed. We each dropped some green stuff on the bill and got up to leave. Walking out, Tad asked me about my love life. The whole thing made him nervous, but he thought heterosexuals ought to bend over backwards to show support for lesbians and gay men. I humored him.

"It's been a busy week...whew!" I didn't mention that all the action was between me and my dual-speed "Reach Easy" electric massage unit with the extra-wide head and the special pleasure ridges.

Tad tugged at his collar with a twitchy finger. "Um. She gotta name?"

"Well," I mused. "There is someone in particular. Rae."

"Ray?"

"R-A-E, Rae. Actually, her name's Tammie Rae. Tammie Rae Tinkers." I blushed. "She's from Smyrna, Tennessee; right outside of Nashville."

Tad was giving me that old Jack Nicholson eyebrow routine. I punched him in the arm. "Give me a break, Greenblatt! Just because you never get any."

He laughed and loped off to his Pontiac. I waved goodbye and slid into Phoebe's car. She was reclaiming it today, so I decided to spring for a rental with some of Olive Jones' money. Maybe Phoebe was right. If I fixed my damn car—or got a replacement—I wouldn't have to keep bribing rental agents when they found out I didn't have a credit card. They could be tough cookies to crack, sometimes.

I dropped the Duster on Ramona Avenue and headed downtown to a rental shop. They gave me a dark red, four-door late model Toyota; perfect for blending in with the Orinda crowd. I drove to my office, parked behind the hapless yellow Rabbit, and shuffled some papers for awhile. Then I re-emerged and headed for the Civic Center. It was 2:45 p.m. I had a long night ahead of me and a little bit of fact checking to do first.

13

I found a parking place on McAllister, around the corner from City Hall. As I walked along the side of the building, I couldn't help but imagine the handgun-toting city supervisor, Dan White, crawling through one of the windows on his way to kill the mayor and Harvey Milk. I hadn't lived here in the fall of 1978, but I could see it with such sickening clarity, just like I could envision the fervor of the riots that erupted the following year when White's lenient sentence was announced. Cop cars were overturned and torched in this very spot.

I hot-footed it around to the front entrance, thinking of all the other demonstrations and candlelight memorials that had taken place down here. I'd been to more than a few in my time.

Now government workers in cookie-cutter outfits were moving briskly up and down the broad steps. I smiled at the ones I thought were secretaries and passed through a metal detector just inside the doors. I made my way through the cavernous gothic rotunda and on to the county assessor's office upstairs. This place was more hectic than the one in Contra Costa County, but I also knew my way around better.

I was checking the parcel maps in no time, looking for data on the Turk Street environs.

I wrote down parcel numbers for the Club Femmes and surrounding properties and waited in line for a while. Finally, I passed the information to a harried clerk in a gingham-checked maternity smock and a lank Susan Dey hairdo. She looked miserable.

She returned with startling news: Club Femmes and several adjacent sites had just changed hands. The sellers were Godfrey Bellinski and some other men whose names meant nothing to me. The buyer was Boom Properties, Inc. The clerk had a list of principal investors, which she handed over with a mournful sigh. I hated to bother her again, but I wanted further information on Boom Properties. She turned out to be very cordial, actually, when I asked for more help. I guess she just hated her job. Made sense to me.

Twenty minutes later, I learned that Boom Properties was a subsidiary of a Nevada hotel corporation headquartered in Reno. It seemed that Boom had an application pending to build a luxury hotel and conference center on the block now occupied by—among other businesses—Club Femmes. I'll be damned.

The list of investors told me nothing. On a hunch, I stopped in at the recorder's office. I spent a lot of petty cash uncovering useless information about a lot of people I'd never heard of. Then I hit the jackpot. N. F. Novacek, one of the investors, was currently married to William Novacek. But a long time ago she'd married and divorced another guy. N.F.'s full name was Nadine Flack Novacek. The records told me she had filed for divorce in 1971; her ex-husband was Jed Marshall Flack.

"It could be nothing, Nellie."

"Sure it could. And Reagan knew nothing about the activities of his senior staff throughout the entire duration of the Iran-Contra affair."

"I get your point." Phoebe sighed into the phone. "Well, I asked around about Flack. Turns out his father was a good old boy in Nevada politics. He—the father—was a high level judge in Washoe County for a lot of years. That's where Reno is."

"So Jed Flack's a kind of junior good old boy?"

I could hear Phoebe chuckle. "I don't know. The word is he rebelled against his dad—moved out of Nevada when things got too hairy between them. Since he's been in public office in California, he's pushed a progressive agenda. Really different from Flack Senior, I hear."

"What's so progressive about real estate ventures? The guy ever hear of gentrification?" I fumed. I had called Phoebe from a pay phone in the basement of City Hall and all I was getting was rationalization and a case of nausea from the sight of dried gum wads stuck to the edge of the phone cubicle.

"Nell." Phoebe was getting irritated, too. "You're right, Flack's a suspicious character. But how can you assume he's involved in this hotel venture just because his ex-wife is? That doesn't give her much credit for being independent."

"Phoebes, I've been in this business long enough to know that coincidences usually mean something!" God, I sounded like a jerk. I tried to calm down, then added, "Besides, he's from Reno. Home of Boom Properties' parent company."

Phoebe let a few beats go by. "Okay. It's still a stretch, but let's assume Jed Flack, Mr. Tenants' Rights himself, is cutting a private development deal on the sly. Why didn't he do a better job of covering it up?"

"Yeah. Maybe he just needed to deflect attention until after the next election." That didn't sound quite right, but who knows? Flack wouldn't be the first politician to abandon his or her constituency for the promise of gold.

Phoebe and I speculated some more, agreeing on one thing at least: our ambivalence over the demise of Club Femmes. The place was no doubt a shithole, but the women made more money there than they were likely to make scrubbing toilets at the Boom Boom Inn, or whatever they were going to call it. Anti-union fervor was rampant among hotel management in this town. I sighed. Things seemed so complicated sometimes.

I decided to make one more call before leaving City Hall. Lydia Luchetti was a pain in the neck, but she came in handy sometimes, too. She was a reporter for the feminist monthly

Re-View, and if she didn't have any dirt on Jed Flack already, she'd be curious to dig some up after I told her what I knew. I'd sic her on him. That way, she'd help with my investigation and still feel indebted to me for giving her a scoop. I smiled grimly—what a sleazy racket.

I knew the *Re-View* number by heart. The digits spelled out A-G-I-T-A-T-E. The woman who answered said Luchetti wasn't in. But when I gave my name, she said Luchetti had left a message for me. I hung on while she searched for it. I was worrying a piece of peeling linoleum with the toe of my boot when she got back on the line a minute later. The message read: "Tell Nell Fury I need to talk to her about Olive."

Yikes. The woman didn't know anything else about it, or where Luchetti had gone. I tried Luchetti at home and at her lover's—no luck. That's all I could do for now. Puzzling over this latest development, I left the building and took off for home, like any other nine-to-fiver burned out after a long day at the office. Only I had extra-curricular plans for later that night—a little moonlighting in Orinda.

14

I cruised past my apartment looking for a place to stow the Toyota. I found one on 15th, then strolled south in search of some supper. There was a busy end-of-the-workday hum in the air; cars zipping along Dolores, people congregating at bus stops or—like me—heading toward the commercial strip of the inner Mission and its numerous shops, bars, and eateries. I loved my neighborhood.

I walked by one of my favorite San Francisco landmarks: the Mission Dolores. You pass through an adobe entranceway into the original 18th century building with its thick, cream-colored walls and Native American ceiling design of orange zigzags. Then you step back to one of the only extant cemeteries in the city. It's full of decrepit headstones and unkempt shrubbery, and features a wonderfully mysterious shrine to the "forgotten dead." Mission Dolores is an oasis of quiet and Poe-like eeriness in the midst of urban bustle. I'd have to bring Rae here sometime.

In fact, maybe she was free for dinner right now. I cut down 16th keeping my eyes peeled for a public phone. There was one halfway down the block, but its cord dangled uselessly from its bashed-in console. I found a booth in working order over on Valencia, though I wondered how I'd be heard over all the booming street noise. It didn't matter. There was no answer. I wandered into a Salvadoran restaurant, picked up a combination plate to go, and made my way back to Ramona Avenue.

A bundle of items was clogging my mailbox—most of it looked like junk. But a thick envelope with Pinky's return address poked out from the stack. I climbed up the staircase feeling suddenly happy. Maybe she'd sent a copy of the community newspaper that publishes her poetry from time to time.

I rounded the stairs onto the top landing, then jerked to a halt. The door to my apartment was open a tiny crack. I set down my bundles and walked gingerly toward the end of the hall. I knew from watching Jamie Lee Curtis in *Blue Steel*—and all those other movie cops—that you weren't supposed to enter a doorway straight on. Instead, you slide in sideways offering the narrowest possible target. That's what I did, holding tight to the wall and reaching for the Louisville Slugger I keep sequestered behind a coat rack just inside the entryway. I couldn't hear a thing. Gripping the bat, I peeked around the corner that opens into the main room of the flat.

A woman was kneeling on the dusty floor, pawing through a bunch of miscellaneous papers stacked in old milk crates in the corner. She hadn't heard me come in. I stared for a moment, taking in her dirty blond braid, starched cotton shirt, and the kind of high-waisted women's jeans that keep their creases in the front and never fade. I couldn't see her face, but she seemed youngish, hunched there like a pretzel.

I hoisted the Slugger and boomed, sounding tougher than I felt, "What the fuck are you doing?"

She gasped, wrenching sideways and knocking one of the milk crates on its side. I was right, she was just a kid—in her early twenties maybe. She shot to her feet, head jerking frantically for signs of an exit.

I stepped forward, sure now that I had the upper edge. She made a whimpering sound. "What's going on?" I said, keeping the menace in my voice.

"I, I..." She couldn't get anything else out.

"Put your hands on your head and turn around!" Jamie Lee would be proud of me. I did a cursory pat down. The woman was unarmed, but I found a bulky set of pick locks jammed in her back pocket. I threw them on a nearby table top and told her to turn around again. When she did, her big green eyes were all brimmed up with tears. She crossed her arms on her chest, trying her damnedest to keep from crying.

"Jesus Christ," I muttered.

"This is my first week on the job," she said. She sunk back onto the floor, twisting the end of her braid with long, bony fingers and fixing me with wet eyeballs. "What am I going to do?"

"What are *you* going to do?! I'm the one with the options here." I flung the baseball bat aside. "Tell me who you are and what you're up to and I'll think about not calling the police." Little did she know I'd never call the cops in a situation like this. Let her sweat a bit.

"You're Nell Fury, right?"

I nodded.

"I'm Darnelle Comey." She tried smiling a little. It made her look really cute, like someone's kid sister caught with her hand in the cookie jar. "Please don't turn me in. I'll leave now. I didn't take anything—"

"Who are you working for?"

She sighed and turned her head to avoid my gaze. I waited. Finally, she reached into her shirt and pulled a card from some hidden recess. Handing it over, she muttered, "I'm with E-Z."

I almost burst out laughing. There it was on her newly minted business card: Darnelle Comey, E-Z Investigative Services. It was an outfit even more cut-rate than Continent West. The kind of place that gives private eyes our less-than-standup reputation. Tad and I were always sharing stories about the antics of E-Z operatives, and here was one now, right in my own living room.

I grinned at Darnelle. "So you're just starting out, huh? Done any credit card repossessions yet? Record checks down at 850 Bryant? Or is it all glamour jobs like this?" I chuckled. I don't know why I was so amused—I guess I was relieved to be dealing with Darnelle and not some bullheaded intruder with a Smith & Wesson.

Darnelle wasn't having that much fun. "Actually," she said, "they just started training me. I'm an intern."

I raised my eyebrows.

"Through a work-study program at San Francisco State. I'm studying criminalistics."

Wow. When I went to school, we wrote essays, solved math problems, and read books by and about straight white men of the Western Hemisphere. Now they were encouraging research into the lives of social deviants like me. I felt honored to be a part of the curriculum.

I said: "So who's your client?"

"I can't tell you."

"Look, Darnelle, I know about client privilege and all that. But you fucked up here. So you better tell me—"

"No, no." She looked frightened again. "I mean, I really don't know. They didn't tell me. They just said to look for any notes you had about..."

"About?"

She sighed. "About a place called Club Femmes."

Apparently French wasn't included in her course work. She pronounced *femmes* like Little had, with a drawn out "s." Darnelle Comey glanced at my papers strewn all around the floor. "I'll help you clean up. I didn't find anything—"

"Forget it. Just tell me what your boss' name is."

It took a little more cajoling, but she eventually coughed up the name Peko Muncie. She begged me not to call him, and I said I'd think about it. I did want to know who cared enough about my probe to hire someone to investigate me, but maybe I could find out another way. Darnelle swore she hadn't been to my office yet; I gave her a stern warning to stay away. I also gave her some free advice.

"Next time Muncie gives you an assignment, find out who you're working for, why they hired you, and what the stakes are. You're more likely to stay out of trouble that way."

Darnelle gripped my hand with a firm shake before leaving. She seemed incredibly thankful. She even asked me to call her if I ever needed an assistant. I laughed, but I let her write her home number on the back of her business card.

Darnelle wasn't so bad, really. She'd been awfully handy with those pick locks, for one thing.

She'd also forgotten them when she scurried out the door—how fortuitous. I was in the market for a decent set that very night. I fiddled with it. Compared to my rinky-dink set, Darnelle's was like a jumbo Swiss army knife with tweezers, miniature scissors, corkscrew, *and* a toothpick. I smiled as I piled all my junk back in the milk crates and restacked them along the wall. Nothing valuable here anyway.

My food had gotten cold, but it still tasted delicious. I wolfed it down while reading Pinky's letter. She had enclosed a poem. It was printed in a mimeographed fanzine-style newspaper, in the upper right-hand corner of the center-spread. The poem was titled "Jackhammer," and included lots of construction imagery and short, staccato expressions of anger. I read it once, then a few more times, smiling all the while. I still didn't get it, but I felt so proud.

Gillian Finer was scheduled to work that night until 2 a.m. I figured Bellinski would be at the Club during prime business hours, too, so I started for Orinda just before ten o'clock. I was wearing a flannel shirt that held pick locks in one pocket, a compact camera in another. The Toyota had a tape deck, so I'd brought along a compilation of pop hits Phoebe had put together. It was high energy music, good for psyching up. Sappy, too. Paula Abdul belted something about loving her forever as I sped once more over the San Francisco-Oakland Bay Bridge.

I parked the Toyota facing downhill a few doors away from the Orinda house. There was more activity in the neighborhood at this time of night, but I just strolled casually along and nobody gave me a second glance. Bellinski's front porch light was on. No cars in the driveway, though, and everything seemed still.

I walked along a crushed stone pathway toward the back of the house. It was a two-story white colonial with few distinguishing features and a lawn that looked like an inky black lake as it sloped away into dense woods. When I got all the way around the house, I noticed a light on in a room off a back patio. It was accessible through the curtained rear door.

I stood in the shadows for awhile, ears tuned to the home's interior. Nothing. There were too many trees back here for any neighbors to spot me. I looked for signs of a security system, but didn't notice one. It was risky, but I'd just have to be prepared to run, if necessary. I worked with Darnelle's tools for a couple of minutes until I heard a satisfying click. The door came loose and I pushed it slowly, drawing a sharp breath as it squeaked on its hinges. I stopped. I still heard nothing but distant sounds of traffic and muted cricket chirps from the woods. I stepped inside and left the door ajar. A light burned from a corner floor lamp, revealing some kind of lounge room with a well-stocked bar and giant TV screen. The place was overheated and smelled vaguely of cologne and fried onions.

Another light was on in a hallway that led off from the room. I headed that way, suddenly aware of a grunting sound that seemed to come from the other side of the far wall.

The noise got louder as I neared an open doorway down the hall. It sounded a little like sex, but very one-sided. I'd been hoping to find evidence of Cate Jones—and maybe her sister, too—in residence here. This was unnerving. I wondered if I could see through the doorway without being spotted. I gave it a shot.

What I saw was Godfrey Bellinski sprawled on his stomach. He was the one making the guttural noises—someone was kicking him viciously all around his upper body. I tried to suppress it, but I must have gasped when I noticed the red puddle oozing from his silver-crowned head and into the blue shag carpet. The kicker whirled on me. It was Olive Jones.

Or was it Cate? I thought of Haley Mills in *The Parent Trap* playing a set of twins scheming to confuse their mom and dad. I thought about Patty Duke, too, in the seconds before I noticed the weapon in Jones' hand. It was a substantial piece of hardware, some kind of .38 perhaps. She waved it in my direction as I dove, hoping to knock her off balance. I missed; she didn't. I always wondered what it was like to be shot, but the moment I felt the searing pain rip through the left side of my body, I realized I would gladly have gone to the crematorium without having had this experience.

Jones leapt over me and was out the door. A wash of vivid colors rose up in front of my eyelids. I was on the floor groping for something to press against my bleeding flesh. It was hard to breathe.

I realized Bellinski was still conscious, one fish-eye staring at me in horror as I crawled to a bedside phone and called in our whereabouts to 911. Right before I passed out, I recognized Olive's alligator clutch wedged under the edge of an armchair. I stuffed it down the waistband of my pants, happy to know which twin it was after all.

15

I was in and out of consciousness for some time after that. I remember being scooped into an ambulance—it felt like a miracle. I think I eked out Phoebe Grahame's name. And I vaguely recall her holding my hand and showering me with reassurances. I suppose they gave me a sedative at some point, because a big black hole came and swallowed me up and obliterated all my dreams.

The next thing I knew, I was gazing at a rectangle of blue, blurred around the edges. I blinked. Everything looked familiar and I suddenly realized why: I was in my own room.

Then I noticed a figure poring over my tiny collection of Favorite Lesbian Novels. She was in a tight black skirt, a white blouse with periwinkle polka dots, and a Ringo Starr cap of hair with blunt bangs and perfectly formed spit curls. It was Tammie Rae Tinkers.

She must have heard me gulp, because she dazzled a smile in my direction and held up a dog-eared copy of Gale Wilhelm's *We Too Are Drifting*. "This any good?" she asked.

"The best." I started to sit up but collapsed again when I felt a prickly numbness meander down my torso. Shit.

I shrugged feebly at Rae and a furrow appeared between her brows. Her lashes were curves of thick black brush, the eyes themselves like a couple of periwinkle orbs that had drifted up from her shirt. Her lips were pinkish and her skin glowed with the alabaster sheen of a well-polished statuette. I thought I might faint again in the face of such a vision.

Rae was shorter than me and a little plumper, but we otherwise shared the same build. Lots of hip, lots of breast, and the kind of strapping musculature that would have made us hits during the Marilyn Monroe era. Rae was a hit with me, just walking across the room to place a cool hand on my forehead.

"Are you feeling any better?" she asked. She perched on the edge of the bed.

"Yes." It came out in a croak. "How did I get here?"

"Phoebe brought you home. She had to go to work so she called to see if I could come over."

I was having a hard time following the sequence of events. "She carried me up the stairs?"

Rae smiled. "Nell. You were awake for awhile this morning. Phoebe said you were talking up a storm, then conked out again." She added, almost as an afterthought, "Phoebe's nice, you know? Not really as tough as she seemed that other time I met her."

I looked out the window again. "What time is it?"

"It's about five. I'm glad you woke up. I have to go soon, myself." She let her hand trail across my cheek, then pushed a tangle of curls behind my ear. I shuddered. We'd never been on a bed together before. She kissed me softly, just the faintest brush of lips.

"I'm glad you're all right," she whispered.

I could feel myself blushing—maybe Rae would think I was feverish. I wiggled a little and realized my left arm was immobilized in some kind of sling. Otherwise, everything seemed intact. I asked, "What happened? Did Phoebe tell you?"

Apparently I'd sustained only a glancing gunshot wound. The bullet had deflected against the camera in my front pocket and grazed my left shoulder. Bellinski was in much worse shape. A bullet had entered his temple, plus he had severe internal injuries from trauma to the upper body. He was in an East Bay hospital in a coma, with only a slim chance of surviving.

I'd been treated at the emergency room, then released after a night of observation. Phoebe had been there the entire time. She'd driven me home this morning during one of my talkative moments, after I'd given the police a brief statement. And here I was. With a bevy of cops on both sides of the Bay eager to grill me even further.

"Phoebe made them leave you alone until you were feeling up to it," Rae explained. "But I guess you were able to name the perp." She smiled to herself, pleased with her knowledge of the lingo. Then her face became grave again. "It was that woman Olive, right?"

I nodded. I closed my eyes for a second, trying to remember as much as I could from the night before. I blinked them open and looked down at the flimsy hospital gown I was sporting. "Rae, do you know what happened to my stuff?"

"You mean your clothes?"

"Yeah."

"No...your shirt probably got torn up. Phoebe said the camera was demolished." Rae gave her head a grim shake.

I sat up quickly, suddenly anxious. The painkillers must still have been working because nothing hurt that much, really, I just felt partially disembodied. At least I'd reinjured the same arm that was already screwed up. I flicked my eyes across the small room. I spied an unfamiliar plastic bag and nudged Rae. "What's that? Can I see it?"

She didn't understand what the big deal was, but she shrugged and went to fetch it. It was my stuff, alright—a thoughtful nurse must have packed it up and given it to Phoebe. My pants were there, a little bloodied, with the pick locks buried deep in a front pocket. Phew, they must have gone unnoticed. The bag also held car keys, underwear, loose change, and the alligator clutch purse. Voilá. I was glad no one at the hospital knew I wasn't the handbag type.

I explained its significance to Rae as I dumped the meager contents onto the bed and started pawing through it. Lots of usual garbage, like tissues and ballpoint pens and a lipstick. Nothing juicy in the way of a date book or a listing of addresses and phone numbers. I picked up Olive's wallet. Rae whistled when she spotted the stash of greenery. It didn't surprise me.

There was a compartment filled with cards and IDs, which I started to flip through. Olive Jones belonged to Triple A, the L.A. Public Library, Blue Cross, the Audubon Society, and one of those clubs in which membership has its privileges. My business card was there, too. So were some old photos.

One was of a smiling middle-aged couple, maybe her late parents. Another could have been the twins at age thirteen or so, standing shyly in unfilled-out bikinis. There was also a photograph of more recent vintage. I gawked. The vivid color snapshot showed Olive encircled in the arms of Godfrey Bellinski, a beautific smile on her face as she gazed into his eyes.

I scrutinized the picture. For a moment I thought it might be Cate, but that didn't wash. The pair was standing in front of the Pacific Palisades home—I recognized one of the yard sculptures. And the commercially developed print was dated August 1989. Cate had already moved to San Francisco then. So Bellinski might be the boyfriend who broke Olive's heart. If so, he then fled north and became her sister's boss. Weird.

I was pretty sure Olive Jones fired at me last night because I surprised her. It was just a reflex, a shot gone wild. I didn't think she'd come after me again. But I was also convinced now that her assault on Bellinski was more purposeful. Was it overdue revenge for his desertion? Or had she discovered an unseemly connection between Bellinski and Cate?

I looked at Rae. "Do the police have any line on Olive Jones?"

"Not that I know of. I think she's still on the loose." Rae peered at me, the worried crease reappearing in her forehead. I smoothed it with my fingertip. She asked, "Do you know what's going on?"

"No." I told Rae what I surmised from the photograph, though, and a little more about the events of the past week. We tossed some ideas around, and I started to work up a fierce appetite. Rae made some impromptu dish out of the odds and ends she found in the kitchenette. It was tasty, full of onions and garlic and some of the spices I have on hand but don't really know how to use. We toasted each other with bottles of A & W.

"I've gotta go, Nell. I'm moderating a meeting tonight in North Beach." Rae was studying environmental engineering at Berkeley, and she also worked as a part-time consultant for the city, organizing neighborhood recycling efforts. When I'd first met her at the Mission site, she'd made a point of pulling a few old gay rags out of my pile of newspapers and asking if she could read them. I never would have guessed otherwise. The sly devil.

Rae left shortly thereafter. As soon as she was gone, I got up to go to the bathroom. The numbness in my left shoulder and arm was mostly gone, though a pounding ache was beginning to take its place. At least it didn't hurt to walk around. I used the toilet, brushed my teeth, splashed my face with cool water, and threw away the hospital garb. I wondered if Continent West would let me stay on its group health plan much longer, what with all the medical bills I'd been racking up lately.

I maneuvered myself into a big ratty sweatshirt that said "Pebble Beach" across the front. It was a knee-length hand-me-down from my brother Harry who worked there as a golf pro. I shoved my matted hair into the faded Cubs cap I keep stashed on a hook behind the bathroom door. I felt like a million bucks; clean, well-fed, alive, dressed in my favorite loungewear with one arm of the sweatshirt dangling free. Then I remembered my mixed-up, hodgepodge of a case.

Rae said she'd turned the volume way down on my phone machine so I wouldn't be disturbed. I went to check it out, turning it up again and hitting the playback button. All the usual suspects had called—Greenblatt, Luchetti, Inspector Little, an Orinda police officer, a couple of impatient clients, and Harry Fury, who must have called our sister because she even called from Minneapolis. The surprises were Mallory Valdez, who asked me to get back to her right away, and a message for Marcia Rhodes from my poodle-toting pal Martha, wondering if I knew why uniformed cops were hanging around Olive Jones' home in Pacific Palisades.

I called Mallory Valdez first. She told me that Club Femmes was closed indefinitely, with Bellinski out and the staff all shook up. She said she'd seen no sign of Gillian Finer. Or Cate Jones, naturally. But she said another friend of hers from work had information that might be useful. Apparently the woman, Lila Groveson, had been frightened and reluctant to talk. Valdez had convinced her to see me, if not the police. I arranged to hook up with Valdez the next day—she'd take me to meet Lila Groveson.

I placed a call to Martha, too, and feigned ignorance about the whole situation. I told her to keep an eye on things, though, and to let me know if she heard from either of the Jones twins. I decided to blow off cops and clients until tomorrow. But I called the number for Cate and Gillian's apartment just in case; like I expected, there was no answer.

Then I spent about half an hour reassuring my siblings that I was fine and everything was cool and, yes, I'd visit sometime soon. Harry and Grace were both good eggs, actually. I twirled the phone cord for a minute, trying to remember the last time we three had been together. Maybe not since our mother's funeral nearly eight years ago in Cleveland. She'd died after a short bout with cancer. My dad was dead, too—he'd been killed in a liquor store stickup when I was fifteen.

Finally, I dialed Luchetti. She snapped up the phone so fast I wondered if she'd been waiting for my call.

"Hi Lydia. It's Nell."

"Did you get a chance to talk to Bellinski before he lost consciousness? Did he say why Olive was after him?"

"I'm fine, thanks. How are you?"

Luchetti snorted. "Since when are you into the social niceties?"

"You're right, I'm a clod. I'm also a cranky clod since I took a slug in the shoulder." Lydia Luchetti had played me for a patsy once and I was a little short-tempered with her. I took a slow breath and remembered how I used her, too, from time to time. It was a mutual kind of thing. I went on: "Sorry, Lydia. I'm just curious what you know about Olive Jones. And how you tied her to me."

"It was just a hunch," she explained. "Your name was mentioned in the paper, you know, in an article about Held's murder. And I was doing a feature on COYOTE. You know about them?"

I murmured yes.

"Okay. So some of the women in COYOTE have been doing AIDS education, you know, great community-based stuff. That was going to be my angle for the story. Then I was talking to this one woman, a prostitute, who told me about a club owner in the Tenderloin. Bellinski, right? Seems he was chatting up some of the sex workers down there, trying to recruit women for a brothel. It irritated her, you know? The COYOTE women, they like to be autonomous, not manipulated by some entrepreneurial creep—"

"But—" I paused, remembering that Mallory Valdez had told me something similar. "How was he going to pull that off? Some surreptitious operation out of Club Femmes?"

"No no. It was all above-board. Legal. He was planning to open it in Nevada."

"Ohhh..."

"Yeah." Luchetti kept rattling on. "It made me curious, you know? Like how was Bellinski going to finance this operation? Can anyone just move to Nevada and open up a whorehouse? So I started poking around. I traced Bellinski back to L.A. and found out about the first Club Femmes—"

"And how it burned down," I interjected.

"Right! You're not so shabby, Fury. So I bet you know that Bellinski knew Joe Lockenwood and probably had a hand in the arson. Then since the insurance fraud fizzled, he needed another way to get fast bucks to open the San Francisco club."

It dawned on me. "Olive Jones."

"That's what I think, too," Luchetti said. "Bellinski courted her, weasled away some of her money, then dumped her. That would be a pretty good motive for a revenge murder, wouldn't it?"

I didn't answer right away. It made sense to a point, but it didn't explain Cate's disappearance. Or why Olive Jones had hired me in the first place, unless she really was just looking for her sister and became incensed when she discovered Bellinski had hooked up with Cate. It also didn't shed any light on how Bellinski planned to bankroll his Nevada enterprise. I wondered how much payola he'd get from Boom Properties, Inc.

Luchetti was needling me. "Nell, what do you think?"

I tried to decide how much to tell Luchetti. She didn't seem to know anything about Cate Jones, or Jed Flack's possible connection, either. Damn. Nevada was sure popping up a lot lately. I said: "Lydia, did you know that Club Femmes and some properties around it have been sold? To a group of Nevada investors who plan to open a hotel there?"

"No!"

"You might want to look into it. It could add to your story. Sex workers displaced from their neighborhood, along with residents and small businesses..."

I liked the grateful tone in Luchetti's voice. So I fed her Jed Flack's name, too, and the information that Flack's ex-wife was one of the Boom Properties investors. This was turning into a beneficial conversation. She promised to tell me if she discovered anything meaty on the city supervisor or his ties to Godfrey Bellinski. In return, I said I'd keep Luchetti informed about Bellinski's progress and Olive Jones' motives or whereabouts. We clicked off.

I hadn't mentioned Cate Jones. I don't know why—I just knew I had to keep looking for her myself. I had this queasy feeling she could tie the whole mess together. I remembered for a moment that I was clientless, vis-a-vis the Joneses, and that none of this was my concern any longer. Then I felt the throb in my shoulder. I'd gone through hell last night; Olive and Cate were no doubt caught in their own ongoing nightmares. Like it or not, this case was still my business.

It was going on 9 p.m. There was one more thing I could accomplish that night. I considered simply phoning Peko Muncie of E-Z Investigative Services, then thought better of it. Darnell Comey had been a good sport, after all. Who was I to screw up her career? A sucker, that's who.

I yanked on baggy pants, dropping Darnelle's pick locks in a back pocket. They had sure come in handy. Rae said Phoebe had retrieved my rental car today and parked it out front. Bless her. There it was, ticket-free, right outside the apartment door. It was a little tricky driving with one arm, but fortunately the Toyota was an automatic. I made it to the E-Z offices and back in under an hour, encountering no difficulties in my new pastime of breaking and entering.

The E-Z client files had offered up one interesting tidbit: San Francisco City Supervisor Jed Flack hired E-Z Investigative Services to find out what I knew about Godfrey Bellinski and Club Femmes. The question was, if Flack and Bellinski were in cahoots, as I suspected, why did Flack need outside help to learn more about Bellinski? Or were they *both* worried that I already knew too much?

16

Everything felt worse in the morning. My arm had stiffened, my chest ached where the camera had exploded against it, and my head was cloudy from lack of sleep. I'd stayed up late reading the night before, wanting to find out if Kinsey Millhone would go to bed with this fellow Dietz. Then I woke early out of anxiousness—whether for Kinsey or myself, I wasn't sure.

It was only six-thirty, but I needed to be alert when the cops came calling. I straggled into the bathroom where I managed to wipe myself down with a soapy washcloth and apply a fresh bandage over my jagged wound. The sling came out crooked when I velcroed it into place; it would have to do. I tossed back three aspirins with a cranberry juice chaser and boiled water for coffee. When the doorbell rang at 7:45 a.m., I was more-or-less presentable in faded khaki trousers and the last clean white T-shirt I could find in the flat.

Orinda had sent two of its finest to get my statement. One was a long, tall Sally who did justice to her well-pressed pantsuit. The other, a garden variety plugugly, had a permanent sneer etched below his cauliflower nose. They spent about an hour playing good cop-bad cop and making a dent in my supply of dark French roast from The Castro Bean.

I told them what I remembered of the shootings, neglecting to explain that I'd busted in without invitation. I just said I was there following a lead on a missing persons case, and mentioned that Inspector Little of the S.F.P.D. could validate my story. I figured they'd already talked to him anyway. Neither of them said so, but it occurred to me that Olive Jones might now be a suspect in the murder of Melvin Held. They tried their theory out on me about Jones' attack on Bellinski—retaliation in the wake of a love affair gone sour. I shrugged noncommittally to that.

I decided to be more forthcoming with Little himself, who I visited later that morning down at the squad room. For one thing, he treated me more respectfully this time, which I'm sure was due to his desire to milk me for information, not out of any concern for my well-being. But also, I realized Little and I were basically on the same track. We both wanted to find Cate and Olive Jones. I was also interested in the possible corrupt business dealings of Bellinski and Jed Flack—but Little didn't have to know about that. At least not yet.

Little told me that Bellinski was still in a coma and Olive Jones still on the lam. He also warned me to steer clear of the situation. I repeated my no-promises shrug. I was getting a lot of practice at that.

The sky was overcast when I stepped back outside. The streets felt bleak today, too, as drab and depressing as the inside of the cop station with its gray decor and perpetually stale air. I didn't really mind. I liked the melancholy tinge of this town. You could go for days without noticing the weather in San Francisco, then a heavy fog would trundle in or the sky would emerge a sudden mosaic of brilliant blue, and you'd remember the natural drama that underscores the edginess of this tiny peninsula clinging to the side of the continent.

I hiked over one block and hoofed it down Polk Street to City Hall. I was supposed to meet Mallory Valdez in an hour and a half. That would give me time to confront my representative in municipal government, Jed M. Flack. Or so I thought.

It turned out I couldn't even get past the stubborn receptionist, much less in to see the supervisor himself. I was offered an appointment with Flack on a Tuesday, three weeks hence. When I responded a little testily, the receptionist hit some kind of button that brought a well-heeled woman bustling out of the bowels of the supervisor's wing.

She treated me to a piano key smile and a handshake more challenging than the bicep curl machine on a Nautilus circuit.

I winced. "Hello, I'm Nell Fury. I vote. It's urgent that I speak with Jed Flack."

"How do you do?" she said. "I'm Constance O'Herlihy, aide to Supervisor Flack. How can I help you?"

"You can't." I whipped out a business card. "It's, ah, rather complicated. A personal matter. I'm sure he'll see me if you give him this."

"I'm sorry, Miz—" O'Herlihy took the card and read it. "Miz Fury. Even if Mr. Flack would want to talk to you—" The condescending tilt of her head let me know what she thought of *that* possibility. "—he's away from the office today. Set up an appointment for another time and I'll let him know you came by."

"Do you know where he can be reached?"

The piano keys disappeared behind a fortress of apricot lipstick. Geez. You'd think these progressive types would gather a more user-friendly staff around them. I took a step sideways to glance over O'Herlihy's shoulder. She followed, like a slightly poky partner at an Arthur Murray dance class.

"He's not here," she repeated, fixing me with a menacing glare. "Will that be all?"

"Oh sure. Just tell him E-Z does it—" I met her eye. "—when he gets back from Nevada."

"How did you know..." She clamped her mouth again and whirled, stomping away into the recesses of the corridor. Well, well. Even the receptionist seemed a little dumbfounded at O'Herlihy's outburst. I raised my good shoulder at him and smiled, then retreated in the direction of the marble staircase.

I felt pretty tuckered out from the rigors of private eyeing. I'd left the car at home, so I caught a bus heading north on Van Ness and transferred to the 38 Geary outbound. I hopped off at Divisadero. There was still time to kill before I was due to meet Valdez, so I mosied along in search of a square meal. I spotted a storefront chicken joint that looked like it would do the trick. I ordered a mini-bucket special: extra-crispy breast, greens, fried okra, and a corn muffin. It wasn't the easiest lunch to eat with one hand, but I did a decent job of it, sealing my fate of an imminent trip to the laundromat.

I was sitting in the window of the tiny restaurant reading a discarded *Chronicle* soiled with chicken grease when I saw Mallory Valdez cruise by in a blue Chevy station wagon with fake wood paneling. We were supposed to rendezvous at the corner of Sutter and Divisadero, just a block up the street. Valdez must have seen me, though, because she promptly walked by the window and waved, frowning when she noted my arm sling. I hurriedly tossed out my wrappings and went to greet her on the sidewalk.

I brushed away her questioning glance with a shrug and said, "Hi there."

"Hi Nell. How are you? My boyfriend lent me his car so I'm a little early."

Funny. She didn't seem like the type to have a boyfriend. You can never tell anymore. I gave her hand a little squeeze and thanked her for arranging this meeting.

"Yeah." Valdez narrowed her eyes. She was still wearing her Levi jacket but now she had a dress on underneath, a wide-skirted affair with a belt and a print of tiny lilacs. It made her look really mature, like somebody's aunt or a member of the PTA. She said: "Lila's been really freaked out. She quit right after Held was murdered...which isn't so surprising...except Lila needed the job real bad."

"Did she say why she quit?"

"No. She wouldn't even talk to me at first. And I was her best friend down there." Mallory Valdez paused, holding me in a steady eyelock. "She didn't get along too well with the white girls. She thought they were crazy for making a big *political* deal out of topless dancing. Not that everyone in COYOTE is white. But you know. Different priorities."

I must have looked puzzled because she continued, "Lila thought everyone in the so-called 'sex industry' was a scumbag. She didn't want to be in a union, or try to reform anything. To her it was hopeless. She'd just work her ass off, collect her pay, and get out of there."

"Did she find another job?"

"I don't know." Valdez fixed her gaze at some distant spot down the street.

"How about you?" I added quickly, kicking myself for being such a jerk.

"I haven't really thought about it yet. I'll figure something out." She tossed her braids. "Wanna go?"

Lila Groveson lived in a housing project on Sutter Street, a few blocks west of Divisadero. There was a stark demarcation line between the gentrified Victorians on one side of the block and the weathered clapboards across the way. The project sat on a sandy stretch of land next to the shell of a triple-decker that must have gone up in flames quite recently—you could still pick up a faint scent of charred wood. We walked across the yard. I followed Valdez into a dank passageway that cut through the center of the beige and green cement building.

Valdez halted in front of a rust-brown metal door toward the end of the hall. She knocked and called out, "Lila?" The hinges creaked open just a moment later. A child of maybe seven or eight motioned us inside, then ran off with a squeal in the direction of a back room.

A compact woman in a black jumpsuit got up from a couch just to the left of the door. She stepped toward Mallory and kissed her on the cheek. Then she swiveled in my direction, a look of measured neutrality keeping her features placid. Lila Groveson had incredibly beautiful eyes, huge, clear ovals of flawless onyx. The rest of her was no-nonsense and spare: close-cropped hair, trimmed nails, minimal jewelry.

I stuck out my hand. "Hi, I'm Nell Fury. Thanks for seeing me."

She nodded, still giving away nothing. I got the feeling she had decided to go through with this, but wasn't very happy about it.

"Sit down here," she said, pointing to the sofa. "I'll be right back."

She walked through a side corridor and I heard the sound of clinking kitchenware. Mallory sighed and took one side of the green velour couch. I sat too. Lila returned momentarily with a pitcher of iced tea and a set of metallic patio glasses.

I accepted tea. Lila sat across from us on a brown leather ottoman and tapped her heels together a few times. "So Nell.

I hear you're looking for Cate Jones." She sipped from her glass, keeping her eyes focused on me over the top of the rim.

"Yes. Actually, her twin sister Olive hired me to find her about a week ago. I did speak with Cate, but she disappeared again. Then I lost track of Olive, too, until the night before last. Did you hear about Bellinski getting shot?"

Lila nodded yes.

I pointed to my left shoulder. "Well, I walked in on it. Olive shot me, too...er, grazed me anyway." A little frown appeared in Lila's forehead as I explained further details about that night. And about my confusion over Cate's whereabouts. "Maybe I'll be able to figure more out if I can talk to Bellinski...that is, if he regains consciousness."

"That'd be a mixed blessing." Finally, Lila smiled.

"I take it you're not too fond of him," I said.

The smile vanished. "It doesn't matter what I think of him. Look, I have some troubles here, you know?" She twisted sideways on her ottoman, taking in the whole dingy room with a sweep of her eyes. I didn't know exactly what she meant by trouble, but I got the basic idea. "Things got a little heavy down at the club. I couldn't afford any more...strife."

"'Heavy' how?"

"Okay. I can't help you much with Cate, but I think I know what happened to old Mel. That's what scared me away. You know how they found his body on, what was it, Monday morning?"

I nodded.

"Well, the day before that, I got to work early. I was sitting out in the alley, you know, by the side door, having a cigarette. It was a nice day. I heard these voices inside, kind of raised up. Not fighting really, just anxious. It was Bellinski and Gillian." Lila looked at me. "Gillian Finer. Cate's girl."

She poured a long swallow of tea down her throat before continuing. "They were talking about Cate and Olive. That's her sister, right, Olive? Something about how they knew Olive was in town but they couldn't find her. How maybe she was 'on to us.' That's how Gillian put it. 'Maybe Olive is on to us.' Makes you think they're scheming something, right?"

"You bet." It didn't surprise me much, but it was interesting to hear it confirmed. Made me wonder if Bellinski and

Finer had penned the note that got Olive to come north. But for what purpose?

Valdez spoke up. "Tell her about the prostitution part, Lila."

"Right." Lila went on, "So then Bellinski said something about a cathouse. And that they couldn't wait much longer on the other properties, either. They needed to 'move forward.' I couldn't hear much, but I caught the word 'risky.' Then the shit hit the old fan. Melvin Held must have been crouched behind the bar the whole time because I heard Bellinski walk back there—I think that's where he went, maybe to get a drink or something—then he screamed out Held's name. Whew, he cussed him out! Then I heard glass breaking, figured Bellinski must be pushing Held around. Gillian was screaming, too. Boy, I wanted to get away from there, I'll tell you that."

Lila was leaning forward now, tapping her heels double-time. She paused to fish a cigarette out of a breast pocket. It was one of those long, skinny ones, wrapped with pale brown paper. "So that's about it," she said, striking a match. "I heard Melvin Held saying, 'I didn't hear nothin'!' He and Bellinski didn't get along, anyway—I don't think Bellinski trusted the guy. There was some more shouting. I decided to scram. Took a walk around the block until it was time to start my shift."

"Then Held turns up dead the next day."

"That's the picture," Lila said. "Two plus two, you know?"

"Do you have any reason to think Bellinski and Finer knew you were there? That you overheard the conversation, too?"

"No. But I didn't want to take any chances. I quit that day."

Mallory Valdez was staring at her friend. I guess Lila had told her about the eavesdropping, but not about Melvin Held's part in it. "Lila..." Valdez couldn't think of anything else to say.

"I know," Lila said. "It's a big fucking mess. And I don't want to have anything more to do with it."

I knew the answer, but I asked the question anyway. "Did you go to the police?"

Lila shook her head, blew a wisp of smoke toward the ceiling.

I let out some air. "Okay. This helps a lot, Lila. Thanks. I'll do my best to keep your name out of it." I set down my untouched tumbler of iced tea. I would've killed for an A & W. Laced with Jameson's, preferably. Nobody said anything for a minute, but I could sense Valdez fidgeting beside me. I cocked my head her way. "All set?"

"Yeah...shit, Lila, be careful, okay?" Valdez hopped up to hug her friend.

"Sure thing." Lila was speaking to Mallory, but she kept her sober eyes focused on me. "I'll be careful. You too, okay?"

17

Mallory offered me a ride but I said no and waved her away in the Chevy wagon. My watch read 3:15 p.m. I stopped at a corner mom & pop for a root beer and picked up a pack of Licorice Whips, too, to give my jaw a good workout. Back outside, everything seemed normal: the sky remained a ceiling of dustmop gray, sirens wailed, a couple of teenagers were harassing women on the opposite corner, fresh pigeon droppings sullied the window ledge I was aiming to perch on.

And Bellinski and Finer had probably murdered Melvin Held.

Where did that leave me? With the same old missing twins I'd been birddogging all along. And a nagging twitch that told me each of them was being played for a sucker. I knew now that Olive had figured it out, at least in part. She was on a vigilante mission to get Bellinski, after all; in fact, she may have already succeeded. But I still didn't know how Cate fit in. Or if she'd fit into anything anymore besides a big pine box.

I sucked on my drink and walked toward Post Street, head down, thinking of all the angles I could explore. I could double-check all of Cate's hangouts, find out if Luchetti had uncovered anything on Jed Flack, start working on Gillian Finer's likely whereabouts, scope out this Nadine Flack Novacek, heck, I could even take a trip to Reno—The Biggest Little City in the World. On the other hand, I could dump the whole can of worms in Little's scrawny lap and get on with my other paltry affairs.

I kicked a cardboard box that was cluttering up the sidewalk and slurped some more root beer. I glanced a second time at my watch. Not knowing what to do, I fell back on a trusty Nell Fury tradition: I decided to take in a matinee.

The Kabuki Theater was on the edge of Japantown, just a short hike east. I passed the site of the old Fillmore West concert hall where Janis and friends had a heyday during the time when people really did wear flowers in their hair. Now the only flowers in the vicinity were withered dandelions straining to find sustenance in cracks that spiderwebbed across the chipped cement.

Like Lila Groveson's, this neighborhood was a study in contrasts. There was a block of decaying buildings with graffitied metal awnings where the doors should have been. Just across the street, a patch of condos popped up merrily like crocuses in springtime. The Kabuki, too, had undergone metamorphosis. Originally a Japanese theater, it became a rock club for awhile, and now was reincarnated as a multiplex picture house with all the charm of the waiting area at the DMV. But no complaints. Once the lights go down, you're still at the movies.

Miami Blues wasn't as good as the book, but it wasn't bad either. I loved the vinegar pie scene and the way the pawn shop woman handled that nasty snickersnee. And Hoke Moseley had so many trials and tribulations it made me feel blessed to be walking around with only a sore arm and a perplexed mind. I felt almost happy when I got out of there. Nothing like an afternoon of playing hooky to KO the blues. Be they the Miami *or* the San Francisco kind.

Phoebe Grahame was sitting on the front stoop when I made it home to Ramona. She was wearing her black and white checked pants and a beat-up T-shirt with "Queer and Present

Danger" stenciled across the chest. She took in my bandaged arm with a flawless poker face and said, "Hey Nellie. Did you hear the Cowboy Junkies have a new record coming out?"

"Cool." I peered into the cellophane bag propped against her right leg. Phoebe was munching her way through what looked like shredded tire bits the color of wet sod.

"Wakame," she said, grinning. "I brought stuff for dinner, too. Are you hungry?"

"Is my name Nell Cather Fury?"

"Oh yeah, Cather. I forgot about that."

My mother had given us all literary middle names. My brother is Whitman, and my sister is Dickinson. Wishful thinking, I suppose. I hadn't had a chance to tell her before she died that she'd picked closet cases for all three kids. I shared that thought with Phoebe.

She laughed. "Good thing! From what you've told me, she'd probably have gone on a campaign of 'outing' Willa Cather."

"What's wrong with that?" I was sick of the "outing" brouhaha already.

"Not a thing," Phoebe replied, still chuckling. Gwen had been a character, alright. She didn't understand it too well when I first came out to her, but then she became a gung-ho member of Parents and Friends of Lesbians and Gays. She went to more Gay Pride marches than I did, and read everything from *Patience and Sarah* to *Sappho Was a Right-on Woman*. I was sorry Phoebe never got to meet her.

I said: "So, about that food..."

I trudged up the stairs behind Phoebe, stopping to pull a thick manila envelope out of the mailbox. There was a note on the outside from Lydia Luchetti. She said she'd enclosed a bunch of xeroxed clips from the *Bay Guardian*, and other papers. I'd check through it later.

Once inside the apartment, I pulled a second chair into the kitchen and plied Phoebe with questions about the hack trade. She told me anecdotes while whipping up a pan full of omelet, heavy on the avocado and cheddar. I let her throw in a little wakame after she explained the merits of seaweed. I'll try anything once. Phoebe drank her usual rotgut red and I made a couple of St. Pauli Girls disappear. We ate our eggs and caught up on the last few days.

"So you don't think Olive Jones will come after you..." Phoebe ended on a high note.

"No. Why should she? I can't do her any more harm—she's already been fingered if Bellinski dies. I think she's lying low, maybe still trying to find Cate."

"I don't get it—"

"I don't either. But suppose Bellinski and Finer conspired to get ahold of the Jones' fortune. To buy up real estate. And maybe invest in the bordello business. That makes sense. With Jed Flack as some kind of middle man."

"Yeah. Maybe Cate's in on it, too."

"I thought about that. But I'm not so sure. I need to find out who stands to inherit if both twins die."

Phoebe rubbed the bottom of her glass up and down her thigh. She always drank wine out of a plain water tumbler, like they do in Italian restaurants. "Nell, this isn't even your case any more. The cops are probably working the same theories you are."

"I know." I wiggled my damaged shoulder. I looked at Phoebe and didn't say anything. She already knew there was no love lost between me and the S.F.P.D. She'd been on the receiving end of my stubborn streak a few times, too.

Phoebe sighed. "Okay. So what are you going to do?"

"Find out what Jed Flack is up to in Nevada. Work on Gillian Finer. You know." My mind was clicking forward. Maybe Finer had Cate holed up someplace...

Phoebe started rummaging through the brown paper bag she'd carried the groceries in. She told me to get busy for a minute—she'd brought another surprise. I got up to deposit the dishes in the sink while Phoebe snuck a package into the bathroom. Whatever.

I sprayed a little water and detergent on the kitchen mess, then went to check my phone machine. Nothing more exciting than a robot-voice inviting me and my spouse to enter a win-an-RV contest. I sat down again and began writing a list of things I needed to do tomorrow.

Phoebe entered the room holding something behind her back. "Close your eyes, Nell."

I hate that sort of thing. I peeked while she placed a clear, shiny object on the fake mantel. I gasped. It was a delicate little fishbowl filled with indigo and black stones and a pair of dazzling crimson fish.

"Phoebe!"

"I thought you'd like 'em. Low-maintenance pets, you know? Just change the water now and then and toss in some of this." She set a satchel of organic fish food next to the bowl.

"Thanks, sweetheart!" I stood up to give her a smack. The fish were zipping in unison back and forth across the tiny basin, like dancers executing some crazy kind of tango. They were beautiful.

"I'll have to name them—"

"I already thought of that," Phoebe said. I watched a glint appear in the corner of her eye. "How about...Cate and Olive?"

I groaned. Phoebe could sure crack herself up. "No, really Nell—" She reached out to smooth the back of my hair. "—how do you like Flannery and Carson?"

"Perfect." We kept smiling at each other until it was time for Phoebe to go home.

I called Rae before I went to bed. She told me I interrupted her studies, but she didn't seem to mind too much. We talked for about twenty minutes, then made a plan to get together the day after tomorrow. I hung up feeling piqued and contented all at once.

Then I dumped the contents of the manila envelope all over the covers and started perusing. Luchetti had dug up political reportage about Jed Flack covering a number of years. There were even a few items dating to his initial run for the Board of Supervisors. *Chronicle*, *Examiner*, and *SF Weekly* clips were mixed in with those from the *Bay Guardian*, though Luchetti must have found the latter most noteworthy. In particular, one intrepid *Bay Guardian* muckraker seemed determined to find something damning about Flack.

But aside from speculation about possible ties to his right-wing father, nothing concrete was cited that would cast doubts on his progressive record. In recent years he'd come out in favor of domestic partner legislation, against the proposed stadium for China Basin, and supportive of efforts to direct earthquake relief funds toward low-income housing. There seemed to be some mystery surrounding Flack's romantic affiliations—he remained resolutely single and had been dubbed a dashing divorcee. We all know what *that* means. So what was the big secret?

I was stuffing the clippings back into the envelope when I noticed a layout of photos from an *Examiner* society page. I took a closer look. They appeared to be pictures of various big shots attending some black tie fundraiser. The third photo down on the right showed Flack all spit-shined and beaming with a fluted glass of bubbly in his hand. A woman and man were in the same shot, smiling over at Flack. I read the caption. "Supervisor Flack with local entrepreneurs William and Nadine Novacek." My word.

So Flack and his ex-wife were at least congenial with each other. From the looks of the snapshot, they were even quite chummy, along with old William, too. Of course, they could have been maintaining face for the camera. And even if they *were* pals, it didn't mean they were doing business together. Still, I remembered from my records check that Nadine Flack Novacek was a San Francisco native. I found it hard to believe that she'd hooked up with a Nevada corporation unless there was some tie-in with her Reno-bred ex.

Lydia Luchetti must have come to a similar conclusion or she wouldn't have enclosed this clip. I'd check with her tomorrow. I dropped the manila envelope on the floor and slid deeper into the twisted sheets. I wondered if I could operate the "Reach Easy" with one hand. I gave it a whirl. I sure could.

18

I took a real shower the next morning, keeping my mashed arm out of the water as best I could. Actually, the gash on my forearm was closing up nicely and the stiffness was almost gone from my shoulder. The bullet tear still felt prickly, but the wound looked clean. I repatched it and decided to forego the sling. I was lying on the floor doing a rudimentary stretching routine when I noticed Flannery and Carson hovering at the side of the fishbowl giving me the wall-eyed once-over. I laughed, delighted, then got up and tossed some fish chow over the side of the rim.

Yesterday's pants weren't standing on their own yet so I pulled them on, along with an old bowling shirt that said "Bob" over the breast pocket. Then I spent a few minutes scrubbing out my oxfords. I was actually becoming fond of the hightop boots, but I missed the molded comfort of my favorite shoes. They were wet but clean when I walked outside a few minutes later.

The rent-mobile was collecting parking violations down at the end of the block. What was it *this* time? I didn't bother to check as I strolled by en route to the It's Tops Coffee Shop.

I'd hang onto the car just a bit longer in case I needed to make a sudden dash for Reno.

I warmed a seat at the counter, waiting for the coffee to cool, and flipped through the *Chron*'s Sporting Green. Not much change in the National League East. Phoebe told me she'd read a review of a new baseball book by George Will— apparently he got hooked on the sport years ago while listening to radio broadcasts from Wrigley Field. He'd been a Cubs fan ever since. Yikes. That's the kind of thing that can ruin your day, like discovering you share a birthday with Dan Quayle or something.

I drank my coffee and soaked it up with an English muffin and side of home fries. I got distracted when a quartet of women came in and piled into the booth behind me. One of them was a lanky number in a soft brown leather jacket and a Sinead O'Connor pate—she kept shoving quarters into the tabletop jukebox. She picked all kinds of treats like vintage Kitty Wells, the Judds, Roy Orbison's "Cryin'." That's what I felt like doing, too, when I heard the husky timbre of her languorous laugh. I dragged myself out of there, but not before flashing her some meaningful eye contact. For a second I thought it worked, then realized she was squinting at the menu board behind me. Oh well. I called, "You can't go wrong with a BLT and a mug of murk," and stepped out into the merciless sunshine.

I decided to visit Tad Greenblatt before heading to my office. He was usually at Continent West on weekend mornings; he preferred tackling paperwork when it was relatively quiet on the premises.

A #8 Muni bus swallowed me up and spit me out downtown at the corner of Kearny and Market. I negotiated a maze of eager beaver shoppers and entered a labyrinthine ground floor hallway half a block down the street. Shallow marble steps led to Continent West's modest spread on the fourth floor. The building, like always, smelled of mildewed sneakers with a dash of rancid yogurt.

Tad was there, all right. He yelled for me to come in and I found him running his hammy fingers across the keyboard of a brand new PC. He didn't seem all that pleased with the equipment and appeared to be deleting as much as he was inputting. "Piece of shit," he finally muttered. Then he reached around and clicked off the power.

I grimaced. "Tad, you're not supposed to turn it off in the middle like that. You probably lost your whole document. You should have saved it, then—"

"Yeah, yeah. How do you know so much about it?" He stood up and gave me an approximation of a hug.

"Pinky taught me. Last time I saw her in London. She's a whiz."

"Pinko! How is that kid?"

"Great. You'll see her soon—she's coming at the end of May."

Tad wagged his head. "Good. You must be missing her."

I cracked half a smile. "Um-hm. So—"

"So how are *you?*" Tad butted in. He didn't look at my shoulder but I knew what he was thinking.

I said I was in one piece and motioned him to a lounge room off in a far corner. I didn't regret leaving the Continent West Detective Agency, but I was partial to these seedy old offices. I plunked down in the royal blue easy chair that looked out over the fire escape and the blistered roof next door. Tad found refuge in an adjacent couch that clashed horribly with his burgundy get-up.

First, to get him in a good mood, I told him about my encounter with a flunky from E-Z Investigative Services. He was duly amused. Then I filled him in on my latest troubles.

"Well—" Tad sighed. "Have you checked on Bellinski recently?"

"Not since last night. A nurse said he was holding steady."

"Not any more. He croaked this morning. About 4 a.m."

"Damn." I thought about it some more, feeling an inexplicable lump rise up in my throat. "Damn!"

"Yeah. No great tragedy, I suppose, but it clouds things up a bit."

I swallowed. "Who've you been talking to?"

"Peanut. He says—"

"Who? What do you mean, peanut?"

"You know. Peanut. Inspector Little."

"Little's name is 'Peanut?'" That brought a chortle.

"Nickname. His real name's Peter. Think about it."

"Jesus Christ. Okay. Since when are you so tight with old Little?"

"Oh, he's been coming around. He's not so bad...these fellows with the flashy badges come in handy, Nellie. You should stop antagonizing them so much." Tad smiled when he said that. He knew we'd never see eye to eye on this score. He went on, "Think any more about carrying?"

I shook my head—we'd never agree on that, either. I figured if I had a gun I'd use it, and that's not something I've ever aspired to do. Tad could poke a million holes in my logic, but I didn't feel like hearing it right now.

"Tad-o," I said. "I've been pretty straight with Little. He tell you otherwise?"

"Naw. He just thinks you're still mucking around where you don't belong." He lifted his double-knit shoulders. "Of course you are."

"Yeah. So what are they working on?"

"See, Nellie, if you had decent relations with the po-lice, you wouldn't have to use me all the time."

"Aw, you'd miss me..."

Tad told me they were hunting for Olive Jones. They hoped to get her for Bellinski, and throw in Melvin Held, too, to satisfy the state. I asked if they were concerned about Cate. Tad said the cops were curious, but not convinced her disappearance had any criminal tie-in. I wondered if it was time to come forth with the suspicious note that drew Olive Jones north in the first place.

I explained what I'd learned about Melvin Held's murder, leaving Lila Groveson's name out of it. "This is what's bugging me, Tad. Say they pick up Olive Jones—the cops'll wrap it up right there. With a big fucking bow. Meanwhile, Cate's probably dead someplace, Gillian Finer walks, and whatever scheme Bellinski was up to just steamrolls ahead." I sprang up. "Maybe that's it. Maybe the cops are protecting their kickbacks. They *wanted* Bellinski's plans to go through..."

"A Nevada whorehouse, right?"

"Uh huh." I paused. "And other deals on Tenderloin property, I think."

"Nothing illegal there, necessarily."

"Yeah, but if it takes murder to finance it—" I stopped. It was time to narrow in on Jed Flack. He might hold the key to this whole nefarious operation.

I headed for the door. "Thanks, Tad, you're a gentleman and a—"

"I ain't no scholar! Get out of here." He gave me a little twisted grin.

I smiled back and hustled down to the lobby. I thought about calling Barbary Coast Taxi Co. to see if Phoebe was within shouting distance, then remembered she was getting off work early today. So I hustled out to the street, shanghaied a Yellow Cab, and sat quietly in the back as we headed for Tennessee and Mariposa.

19

I hadn't been to my office since last weekend. Shoot, I was probably missing all kinds of chances to serve subpoenas and shadow wayward spouses. It was weird, I still had that big chunk of dough from Olive Jones, but it smelled like hush money to me and I didn't know what to do with it. I better start getting my affairs in order no matter what happened with the twins.

Mary must have been painting up a storm in recent days. When I walked through the warehouse door, a wall of chemical odor and stale cigarette smoke came up to meet me. Mary was a two-pack-a-day gal, Camel straights. More if she was on an artistic binge. I eyed the fresh canvases leaning against the right wall. They looked like Rorschach blot tests that got caught in a junior high school cafeteria food fight. Nifty.

My little corner was as spartan as usual. Mary had piled some mail on the edge of the desk—I gave it a quick leaf through, pulling out a few items to deal with right away. Then I sat at the typewriter and composed some notes on the Jones case. I had no client to report to—no need for an official write-up—but it helped me organize my thoughts anyway. Finally, I dug out my file box of Important Phone Numbers and thumbed through the Ws.

Emily Winkmeyer was a change-girl at a Reno casino. I'd met her some years back, at the San Francisco premiere of *Desert Hearts*. She was an extra in the film; I was just an avid movie-goer. We'd begun an affair that night—nothing as spectacular as Cay and Vivian's, but decent just the same—that we still rekindled from time to time. I'd never called her before for a professional favor, but I knew Emily wouldn't mind. She got a big kick out of my line of work.

I swiveled to rest my heels on the dusty radiator and punched some digits. The phone rang a bunch of times and I wondered if I was calling too early. Emily worked late hours. Then a groggy voice came on the line.

"Is that the Wink-master?" I asked.

"Hello? Nell?"

"Yeah, hi, it's me."

"Darlin'...my lady p.i.!"

"Well, you got the last part right, anyway. How are you, Em?"

"Ohhh, I'm dead. Can you hang on a sec?"

"Sure."

I heard her clank down the receiver. A minute later a toilet flushed. Then she was back.

"Hiya Nell. Are you in town?!"

"Naw. I wish. Listen, I need your help on something. Do you have some time to talk?"

"Yeah. What's up?"

"Well, it's about the prostitution business—"

"Huh?"

I chuckled. "I'm not planning to moonlight, Em, I just need to know how it works in Nevada."

"Oh..."

"For example, I'm wondering how it's regulated. I mean, can anybody just open a house of prostitution?"

"Well." Emily must have paused to fire up a smoke. She sucked in and said, "It's kinda complicated. You know it's illegal in some parts of the state, right?"

"Umm...you better start from the top."

"Okay. Prostitution's illegal in, let's see, Washoe and Clark Counties. And Douglas, too, I guess. That means no go in Reno and Vegas. But right outside of town, as long as it's over the county line, you can do it. Like, you've heard of the Mustang Ranch?"

"Yup."

"It's got things kinda sewn up around these parts. The Mustang's out Highway 80, just east of town. Gaudy fucking place, like a Disneyland for johns."

"So, what? The Mustang Ranch has a monopoly?"

"Well, in effect. Or it used to, until the owner went on the skids. The IRS took over for awhile—can you believe it?" Emily explained that technically, nothing stopped a newcomer from going into business. But an old boys network controlled operations throughout the state making it virtually impossible for outsiders to break in. According to Em, the system was oiled with regular payoffs from brothel owners to politicians.

I asked why that would be if the businesses were legal.

Emily said: "Oh, they scratch each other's backs, you know. You see, it's all a little vague. Each county regulates prostitution as they wish—any whorehouse can be closed down as a public nuisance, even if it's in a supposedly legal county. So you want your business to fly? Maybe you pay off a judge, a D.A., a sheriff."

"So you're saying it would be hard to compete with the Mustang Ranch?"

"Oh...I think so. Though it's hard to say what will happen now. And it might be a little more open down south, outside of Vegas. I don't know." I could hear Emily striking another match. "What's this all about, Nell?"

"I'm trying to figure out what a couple of entrepreneurs are up to. Em, you ever hear of a company called Boom Properties, Inc.?"

"No..."

"How about a Reno judge, name of Flack?"

"Sure. Old Judge Flack. Talk about the old boys network."

"Hmm?" I dropped my feet to the floor and arched my back.

"Flack's retired now but he was, ah, influential in his time. Probably still is."

"Did you know he has a son, Jed Flack, a San Francisco city supervisor?"

"No. Why?"

"I was just wondering if his name ever came up, in terms of business in Reno or anything."

"Not that I know of." Emily let out a long breath. "Nell, why don't you come out for a visit? Do your investigating up close, you know?"

I grinned. "Thanks, babe, I might do that."

After we rang off, I tried Luchetti. No luck.

So I reached for the San Francisco directory. Jed Flack lived on Connecticut Street, probably just up the road from my office, only his house was on the ritzy part of Potrero Hill. I love it when they're listed. I cleared my throat and dialed his number.

"Hello?" The guy gave it an enthusiastic lilt. Shit, I wasn't ready for this.

"Hi." I tried to sound chipper, like a racquetball pal from City Hall or something. "Is Jed there?"

"No, he won't be back until tonight. Can I ask who's calling?"

"Oh no, I'll just try him at work another time." I hung up fast. Then I leaned forward and rested my chin on my hands.

A minute or two later, I sat up straight and lifted the receiver again. This time I called the office of the National Center for Lesbian Rights. Just an answering machine. Rats.

I wanted a legal tip on how a lesbian might arrange to have her money left to a lover in the event of her death. A regular will, I suppose, would be the most straightforward way, though I know outraged families sometimes contested the wills of lesbians and gay men. That was part of the impetus behind domestic partnership legislation. Hmmm.

It occurred to me Gillian Finer might have conned Cate Jones into some kind of legal arrangement. Maybe Finer planned to nab Olive's nest egg, too. Then she and Bellinski could use the money—and Flack's Nevada connections—to lay the groundwork for a prostitution setup. And other ventures, perhaps. But what would Flack stand to gain? And now that Bellinski was dead...

I scuffed my shoe across the floor a few times, musing on the ins and outs of this theory. It was only then I noticed that my bottom desk drawer was unaligned with the one above it. I gave it a tug. The cheap lock was mangled, hanging limply out of commission. The drawer's contents lay scattered in disarray. I figured out in a flash that the typewritten note to Olive Jones was missing. So was the handkerchief I'd lifted from the apartment off 17th Street.

There'd been nothing wrong with the locks on the warehouse door when I entered. At least nothing obvious. I was getting up to check them when an unexpected visitor barreled in. The locks would need fixing now, that's for certain, judging from the way the lead-footed lubber smashed the door open with his boot and came ambling through, hardware leading all the way.

20

I halted. So did Leadfoot. He sent an unctuous little smile in my direction as I stared down the nose of his gleaming semi-automatic. It was fitted with a silencing device.

"We're going this way, lady," the man said, kinking his head to indicate the entranceway. I was still frozen. He crooned, "Whatsa matter? You don't like guys to open the door for ya?"

Oh god. A regular Andrew Dice Clay. I forced myself to take a few measured steps, keeping my eyes trained on his pistol hand. He wore a natty leather glove with holes cut to let the knuckles pop through.

I took a shallow breath and checked out his face: a pasty oval with a squashed-in crown, sort of like a jack-o-lantern gone to mold. I tried to imagine triangles in place of his eyes and a jagged gash from ear to ear—anything to keep the fear at bay.

"What do you want?" I monotoned.

"You're Nell Fury, am I right?"

No point in denying it. I nodded.

He blurted: "I want *you*!"

"Yes but—" I strained to think of a way out, some kind of stunt to pull. I moved forward cautiously. Maybe there'd be people in the street...

Leadfoot was losing his sense of humor. "Let's go, lady." He gave me a quick frisk, then shoved me with his left hand. I went tripping out the door. Of course there was no one on Tennessee; nobody ever strolled this neighborhood. Shit. For a moment I thought Mary might stop by soon and know something was amiss when she saw the busted door. Then I remembered she was never out of bed before 5 p.m.

I felt Leadfoot lumbering close behind. He was nudging me toward a slate gray sedan parked at the curb, dwarfing my stranded Rabbit. I wondered how he planned to drive and handle the piece at the same time. I didn't see anyone else in the car.

"Hey, hold up." He tapped my arm with the edge of his silencer. I felt a jolt of nausea. "Before we go for a ride, Armand wants you to know something. We've got Phoebe."

Something clamped shut deep down in my guts. "What—"

This time his smirk really did look like a zigzag wound. "Your *girl*-friend. Phoebe. We're holding her, you know, like an insurance policy. You talk, she's fine. You don't—" He shrugged.

"God damn you!" I jerked my head. My fists were dry as chalk, clenching spasmodically at my sides.

"Hey hey hey. We're going to see her right now. Her and Armand. So just shut up, okay?"

He gestured me into the sedan's back seat. Somebody had rigged it like a cop car—no inside door handles, a metal grillwork separating the back from the front. The man got in and cranked the key. Before we took off, he told me to avoid any attention-getting tactics, for Phoebe's sake. I realized I was crying as we pulled away down Tennessee Street.

If Leadfoot ever tired of being a hoodlum, he could carve out a dandy career as a tour bus driver. He took me through the Mission, across Market, up the back side of Buena Vista Park, and down into the Haight, all at an easy sightseeing pace. At one point he actually said, "Nice town, Frisco. Don't get up here too often." I was regaining equilibrium by now, trying to figure out who the fuck Armand was. And what information he could want from me.

We cruised along Waller into the east end of Golden Gate Park. Leadfoot seemed to get lost. I heard him muttering under his breath, then he swung a few wild turns. I recognized the entrance to the Japanese Tea Garden. It was lovely here, really. I tended to forget about Golden Gate Park, unless I happened to pass by en route to someplace else. I tried to think about neutral things, like whether Pinky would still enjoy going to parks. I felt my eyes get all clogged up again with tears.

We were on JFK Drive now, passing by the buffalo pen. A few minutes later I spotted the refurbished old windmill off to our right. Then we turned north onto the Great Highway. Jesus. Where were we going? I wondered if they really had Phoebe, if Armand existed, or if this was all just some ruse to dump me off the tip of Land's End.

The road was crawling with vehicles as we neared the Cliff House. Leadfoot suddenly veered left, cutting in front of oncoming traffic and slipping into a parallel slot just vacated by a trio of motorcycles. The driver pointed his beady eyes my way. "This is where you behave now, or your *girl* ends up in big trouble." He clumped out of the car and opened the back door.

I heard the sound of waves crashing and excited tourist babble. It was a sparkly spring day out there, sun glinting brilliantly off the pavement. I wished I had my sunglasses. I puffed out some air and eased out of the car.

We walked up the gradation toward the Cliff House arm in arm, the moment marred by the gun barrel poking surreptitiously into my ribs. We didn't speak. I tried to figure out why he'd bring me to such a populated area. Maybe Armand was a sucker for touristy hot spots. Heck, maybe they'd take me to Pier 39 when we were all done here.

We bypassed a couple of souvenir outlets and a fast food stand. My stomach growled. Leadfoot steered me toward the Cliff House main entrance. I tried casting panicked glances at some of the dawdlers, but nobody caught on. We went into the showy restaurant and headed due left toward an airy cocktail lounge with broad windows overlooking the Pacific.

The whole room was awash with festive colors: the expansive green-blue of the ocean, the neon leisure wear of tourists, the walls with their swirling floral designs. And there was Phoebe, looking ghost-like in a distant corner.

I skipped a heartbeat or two, then took off in her direction. Leadfoot was right with me. Phoebe saw us coming, but held her motionless pose. The fellow at the table with her stirred, though. He cast a few thousand watts in my direction and stood to greet us. I noticed he had an arresting combination of burnished brown skin and ice blue eyes.

"Well! Monty, Miss Fury...how nice of you to come."

I ignored his outstretched arm. "You got a last name, Armand?"

The eyeballs got wider, then slid sideways at Monty. He chuckled. "Laws. Armand Laws. Won't you sit down?"

We did. I said in a loud voice: "Are you okay, Phoebes?"

She smiled with a pair of lips chewed ragged and said, "Yes." She was usually never chapped. Then I saw that her pupils were hugely dilated. Good, maybe she had a healthy dose of adrenalin flowing. Unless...

"Nel-l-l," trilled Laws. "Care for a drink?"

Jesus Christ, what did he think this was, a double date? Armand and Monty, a couple of jokers all coifed and tucked like a lounge act at the Ramada Inn. And Phoebe, still proclaiming "Queer and Present Danger." Plus me, "Bob."

I started to order soda, then had a change of heart. "I'll have a Tanqueray martini, high and dry. Extra olives." I didn't really want to drink it, but it'd be nice to hold on to.

On command from Laws, Monty sidetracked our waiter. Meanwhile, Laws planted his elbows on the tablecloth and fiddled with a chunk of gold on his left ring finger. "Well now, we're all comfortable. I imagine Monty gave you our, ah, little ultimatum. You just be straight with me...ha ha...in a manner of speaking—"

What a comedian.

"—and everything comes out fine. In fact, Joe kinda likes your style. He says you ever come to So Cal, maybe he has some work for you—"

"Joe?"

"Joe. Lockenwood."

Joe Lockenwood.

"I tell him, maybe you're a little too square. Joe says, naw, he needs dames—"

"I thought Lockenwood was still at Tehachapi."

"Sure he is," Laws said. "That doesn't hinder him too much."

Our round of drinks arrived. Mine was a cold funnel of shimmering simplicity. I took a tiny sip after all and fished out two olives. I handed one to Phoebe.

"So you work for Lockenwood?"

Laws' smile cut a horizontal swath from dimple to dimple. "We work together. Joe's gonna walk soon, and we had some, ah, projects in the planning stages. Along with Godfrey Bellinski. You know about old Godfrey?"

I moved my head up and down. I noticed Phoebe squinting, as if she were trying to put it all together. Monty was looking out the window, glass of beer in his meaty paw.

Laws continued, "Yeah, Joe was upset when he heard about it. He's wondering what's gonna happen to our plans now, what with Bellinski in the ground. So he suggested I come up here, take a look around. I always did like the Cliff House." He tucked into a finger of bronze liquid. "Joe thought I should start with you."

I paused. "Why me?"

"Nel-l-l, you underestimate yourself. Your name was in the papers when Held bit the dust. Just a small mention, but then what do you know? 'Nell Fury' all over again when Bellinski gets iced. A private eye on the scene? A coincidence? Hmm. Joe sends out some feelers, decides you're...umm...in the know."

I placed both hands around the base of my drink. "Fine. Let Phoebe go. Then we talk."

"Ha ha. You got that ass backwards. Ha ha ha."

Monty was grinning with his ridiculous pumpkin face. I scowled his way, then turned back to Laws. "Okay. Here we are. What do you want to know?"

"We've lost track of Gillian Finer. Bellinski's friend. She kinda holds the key right now and—" Laws shrugged, "—we just need to let her know we still want to do business with her.

117

We think you know where she is. Maybe those Jones girls, too."

I didn't believe him for a minute. If they were really looking for Finer, it was probably in order to get rid of her. They'd clean up their messy tracks, then salvage what they could of their money-making plans. I also doubted Phoebe and I would be allowed to just walk away after this little *tête-à-tête*.

Shit. Even if I wanted to play along with Laws, I had no idea where Finer or the Joneses were.

I said: "I have no idea where Gillian Finer is. Or the Joneses."

Armand Laws wagged his head back and forth. "This is unfortunate. Tsk tsk. Hmm..."

Monty finally spoke. "She's bullshittin'."

"Yes. Hmm." Laws started twirling his ring again. "So I guess we need to be a bit more persuasive—perhaps in a more, shall we say, *intimate* setting."

"Won't matter much," I said, feeling that knot of bile kick loose again inside me. I wondered what would happen if I grabbed Phoebe and tried to bolt. What could they do? As if to remind me, Monty gave my knee a few firm taps underneath the tablecloth with something cold. I kicked his shin and said to Laws, "Have you been rummaging through my desk?"

He looked bemused. "Ha ha. Stalling, eh?"

"You betcha. So. You fellows have some business plans, eh? Why don't you tell me about 'em." I drank some gin. I don't know why I was suddenly so cocky; just grasping for time, I guess. I could feel Phoebe's giant pupils impaling me from across the table.

Laws smirked. "Whoa boy. Plans. Joe Lockenwood eats, drinks, pisses plans. But maybe you know too much about them already." He stood up, good humor evaporating abruptly from his sculpted face. "You want to take another stab at the whereabouts of Miz Gillian Finer?"

I hunched my shoulders and kept my mouth shut.

Laws gestured at Monty who sprang up and threw a pile of bills on the table. I took a final swallow and reached for Phoebe's hand. Her grip felt strong. Laws grunted and we moved out in tandem, a couple of rods pushing along those of us who felt reluctant.

Down below the Cliff House, a variety of natural and not-so-natural attractions drew hordes of tourists and weekend idlers. There were coin-operated viewing glasses to look out at Seal Rock, a giant square walk-in camera, a parks information center, and a saltwater-dampened area of ruins where the Sutro Baths were situated at the turn of the century. There were also myriad footpaths leading to a region of scraggly brush and rocky shoreline that wends around and melds with Lincoln Park. Plenty of places to get lost down there, and that's where we seemed to be heading.

I guess I'd blown the job offer from Joe Lockenwood. I felt my armpits get all clammy and knew I had to do something fast. There were fewer people around us now. Despite the sunshine, a wet breeze made me shiver in my shirtsleeves and froze the sweat on my skin.

I staged a trip and went sprawling to my knees. Monty said, "Fuck," and bent to grip my upper arm. I met him with a hard elbow to the groin. His gun went clattering down a rocky incline. A pace in front of me Armand Laws whirled and I looked into the barrel of a spiffy fist-sized revolver.

I flashed on Tad and our ongoing "to carry or not to carry" conversation. Maybe I should at least think about a strap-on ankle knife. Wondering if it was too late, I saw Phoebe lunging up behind Laws. Then a crack resounded from up above us. Before I even registered that it wasn't me who got shot, I noticed a dark stain spreading across Laws' right thigh. He went down, dropping his piece on the way. I booted it out of reach. Monty, crouched and grimacing beside me, looked at Laws with terrified bug eyes. I clobbered Monty in the jaw and scooted frantically in Phoebe's direction.

She was quaking but unharmed, pointing back up the trail toward the Cliff House. I turned to look. A leggy blond woman in huge tinted glasses was scampering toward us. The sun was blurring my vision, but I thought I saw her slip a hunk of shining metal into her jacket pocket. "Come on!" she yelled, when she got within hearing distance. I blinked at her, at Phoebe, at our injured escorts writhing on the rocky soil. Then I blinked double-time when the woman got abreast of us.

It was one of the Jones twins, sporting a platinum page-boy wig. Olive? If so, this woman was too much. First she paid for my services, then she tried to evade me, next she used me for target practice, and now she was gunning to save my life.

21

We were sitting in an orange vinyl booth near the rear of a coffee shop on outer Geary. We made quite a trio: Phoebe chomping nervously on ice cubes from her water glass, Olive Jones slurping cup after cup of brownish-gray muck bleached with artificial creamer, and me devouring a meatloaf special that came with a salad and fries. I guess other people lose their appetites under stress. Not me.

We had scurried away from the scene back at the Cliff House as curious onlookers started flocking toward the sound of the gunshot. Nobody seemed to notice us in the crowd. Phoebe thought we should have stayed. She was furious at me. And at the world, too, I suppose.

I agreed with Phoebe, actually—plenty of people would I.D. us as Armand and Monty's companions inside the cocktail lounge. The law would be on to us shortly. But I wanted to talk to Jones first, and this might be my only chance. She seemed to want to talk to me, too. So the three of us fled in a car Jones had acquired, courtesy of Avis.

The first thing I had said as we zoomed down Geary was, "You *are* Olive, aren't you?"

She had nodded yes.

"What the hell were you doing at the Cliff House?"

Turns out she'd been waiting near my office to shadow me—she thought I might eventually lead her to Cate. Nutty logic, but a lucky break. She'd been right on Monty's tail all the way across town, hovering in the background when we got to the Cliff House, anxious to see what would happen next.

Now she sat opposite me and lowered the silly plastic spectacles with her trigger finger. "I'm so sorry about the other night, Nell. I didn't mean to shoot. I didn't even know who you were! I was just so...enraged." She pulled off the glasses and let her eyes flit fitfully around the restaurant.

"Goddammit," I said, around a forkful of meatloaf. Then I vented some rage of my own. After chewing her out for a while, I eased back with a wheeze and rested an arm around Phoebe's shoulders. She squirmed. I dunked a fry in a puddle of Heinz. "So what's going on, Olive?"

I could barely hear her response. "Do you know where Cate is?"

Gee whiz, *deja vu.* I just said, "Uh uh."

Olive Jones didn't weep this time, but she had trouble controlling her voice. She told me she'd been looking for her sister all week, and was convinced Cate was still in jeopardy. I'd been right on a few counts. Olive and Godfrey Bellinski had been lovers in L.A. Then he'd left her with a battered heart and a depleted bank account to try his hand in San Francisco. Last weekend, when Olive began poking around in Cate's affairs, she found out her twin was working for her ex-flame.

"I couldn't take it," she explained, "it was so despicable. It made me sick that he would ingratiate himself to Cate—she knew he was a creep, how could she fall for that?! And it got me even more worried. Godfrey went a little, I don't know, *crazy*, you might say, after he met Joe Lockenwood. I figured the two of them were up to something. Like getting Cate's money."

There was a hollow tone in her speech I hadn't noticed before. Olive bounced her glasses on the tabletop and lifted her coffee cup. A faint brown moustache was visible on her upper lip when she set it back down.

I said: "So you know about the arson? In L.A.?"

"Uh huh. I mean, I didn't know at the time that Godfrey was connected. But it makes sense, the timing of it. Christ..."

"You know those two guys back there on the rocks? Armand Laws and Monty somebody?"

"Um..." Olive's eyes got panicky all of a sudden, as if she just realized what she'd done. She blurted, "No, I mean I never met them. But Godfrey mentioned Armand's name sometimes. I think. God, I wonder if he's okay, I'm sorry—"

"Hey, no, I'm grateful, really." I rolled my eyeballs. "But they were looking for Cate, too, and Gillian Finer. You know about Gillian—Cate's lover?"

"Yeah."

"Then we're *all* trying to find the happy couple. The thing is—" I searched for a tactful way to say this. There wasn't one. "—what makes you think Cate hasn't been in on some scheme with Finer and Bellinski? You know, like she's hiding out...on purpose...and they plan to kill you?"

"No...uh uh..."

Phoebe got up abruptly and pointed herself toward the bathroom. I could tell she was baffled and really angry. Who could blame her? I wanted to trot after her, but I made myself pay attention to Olive.

"Cate wouldn't do that!" she was saying. "She's the only one I've got left—"

I interrupted. "She lied to me, Olive. Cate told me you had gone home, that everything was fine. She tried to pay me off—"

"No." A fierce blush took over her face. "That...that was me at The Box. I...was just pretending to be Cate. I had made up my mind to...to..."

I gawked at Olive Jones, my knuckles white as I gripped the edge of the table.

She tucked her chin against her chest and whispered, "...to kill Godfrey. If he wouldn't tell me what was going on, I was going to...murder him. And that's what I did."

The story tumbled out after that. Olive Jones said she had hired me in good faith, then tried to trick me into pulling out when she learned Bellinski was involved. She hoped to get away with murder, literally, and thought it would be easier without a private investigator nosing around. But that was all screwed up now, and she was still deathly afraid for her sister. She told me she'd been holed up in a Lombard Street motel, determined to keep hunting for Cate.

Phoebe came back to the booth as Olive was explaining what happened that night in Orinda. Apparently Bellinski had told her Cate was at the house. He had convinced her to go out there, then when Olive discovered it was all a sham, she'd turned on him. Bellinski hadn't expected her to have a gun; in fact, he'd probably planned on killing *her*. And nobody had figured me into the bargain.

Then Olive had uncovered a real bombshell. When she called her lawyer in Los Angeles, the woman said Cate had recently contacted her about changing her will. The lawyer recommended Cate contact a San Francisco colleague. Olive pulled the identical twin masquerade again, visiting the other attorney and gaining access to Cate's will. The new provisions left everything to Gillian Finer, with the exception of the Pacific Palisades property, which the twins held in joint tenancy. In the legal documents, Cate referred to Gillian as her "domestic partner."

"So that's that," Olive said. She guzzled some more joe. "They were going to kill her."

"And you, too," I muttered. I asked Olive if her money went to Cate in the event of her death. She said yes. I realized Cate Jones might well be alive. They may have wanted to maximize profits by disposing of Olive first, and keeping Cate captive until all the money fell to her. Feeble plan, legally, but they might have hoped to capitalize on the growing climate of political respect for domestic partnerships in San Francisco. Or, Cate might be a willing participant in the whole sordid scheme. I kept that thought to myself this time.

I glanced sideways at Phoebe. She must have splashed her face with water in the bathroom. A fringe of hair was spiked wet in front and her shirt collar clung damply to the base of her neck. She gazed back at me with level eyes. She'd ordered a cup of tea which she blew on steadily before venturing a taste.

"We'll be ready to go soon," I said.

Phoebe nodded.

I volleyed a little more information back and forth with Olive Jones. She said she knew nothing about an alleged Nevada prostitution gambit, or about any of Bellinski's plans for the Tenderloin. She didn't seem that interested, either, just agitated about her sister's well-being. I asked if there were any Jones family hideaways where Cate may have gone or been taken—nope. Nor could she think of any other places Cate would likely be.

I dumped my greasy napkin on my plate and pushed it forward an inch. "I owe you some money, Olive."

"What?" she said. She was tugging on a strand of her wig, causing the whole mop to lilt forward.

"All that green stuff. Remember, at The Box?"

It was apparently the last thing on her mind. Olive hunched her shoulders and said, "Oh. Just cover the bill. We're fine."

I glanced at the check. $8.59. Even counting the tip and this week's wear and tear, I was coming out way ahead. Except, I suppose, in the job satisfaction category.

Olive got to her feet and hitched her shades to her nose. She resumed her nervous perusal of the coffee shop, no doubt preparing to slink out.

I didn't feel like stopping her. But I said, "Take a trip to the police station, Olive. Plead self-defense on Bellinski— heck, they might even buy it."

"No, they won't..." Olive Jones was all teary again, behind her violet lenses. I almost felt sorry for her.

"Okay," I said, "but let me know where you're staying. In case I need you."

"Are you going to keep looking? For Cate?" There was a pathetic strain of hope behind her agonized words.

I blew out some air and repeated my now-familiar non-committal shrug. Olive scribbled something on a matchbook and dropped it on the table. "Nell," she said, "I took that letter from Cate. And the handkerchief. You know, from your desk? I didn't want them...floating around."

Shit, I'd forgotten all about that. "How'd you get in?" I demanded.

"That artist let me in last night. I saw lights on and...I just fooled her. She thought I was your friend. I told her you needed something out of your desk. Sorry—"

"Cut the apologies," I snarled. There went all my sympathy. "Just go, already."

Olive Jones tripped out the door. I turned sideways. "Oh, Phoebe—"

"You are just too fucking much, Nell Fury." I was glad to hear the piss and vinegar in her voice. She reached over for a spare french fry that was molded to the side of my plate.

"You're okay?" I asked.

"Oh, just dandy. I always wanted to play out a scene from 'The Streets of San Francisco.'"

"Ummm, I thought it was more like 'Charlie's Angels.'"

Phoebe glared at me. I punched her lightly on the arm, but she wasn't ready to laugh just yet. She made me explain the parts of our recent encounter that she hadn't followed. And she told me how Armand Laws had abducted her as she left the Barbary Coast Cab garages over on Army Street.

"What now? Are you going to the cops, Nell?"

"No, not yet. I've got to make a housecall. Or two."

Phoebe said: "You're crazy. Can't they nail you for aiding and abetting? Or whatever you call it?"

"Naw."

She was right, though. I wondered how Armand and Monty were faring. The cops would want to talk to me, that's for sure, but I planned to stay a few steps ahead of the game. I was too riled up to let go of it now. Curious, too, about Flack and his possible involvement. Besides, I needed to crack this thing and get Joe Lockenwood off my tail for good. He wouldn't be too happy when he heard what had happened to his muscle.

Phoebe was still fuming. I took her hand and asked if she wanted to stick with me tonight.

"No way." She let out a heavy sigh. "I'll be fine. They'll be looking for you, not me. Besides...I've got a date. If I can still get up for it."

I raised a brow.

Phoebe pulled her hand away. "With Johnnie Blue."

Johnnie Blue was a stand-up comic who'd drawn me into the investigation at the AIDS Treatment Clearing House. We became friendly and I introduced her to Phoebe. Johnnie Blue was a fine performer and exceptional in other ways, too, if you asked me. I nudged Phoebe. "Is this a *date* date?"

She finally smiled. "As opposed to?"

"You know, a *friend* date."

"Ohhh." Phoebe ran a hand through her soggy locks. "It's definitely a *date* date."

"Phoebe Grahame!" I thought Johnnie Blue was strictly hetero. That's the impression she gave me when I tried to finagle my own date with her.

Phoebe was chuckling. "Aw, Nell, don't be sore, some of us just have that special touch..."

I left some dollars on the tab, snatched the matchbook with Jones' motel info, and followed Phoebe out to the sidewalk. I guess her anger was thawing. She took ahold of my arm and scanned the street in both directions. It was getting on toward late afternoon. A silky mist hung faintly over the sun-bleached pavement.

Phoebe asked: "Do you ever have fantasies of hitting the road? Just taking off, without a plan. You know, like Bonnie and Clyde?"

"All the time." I smiled. "Bonnie and Bonnie."

Phoebe gripped me a little harder. "Yeah, that's it. Bonnie and Bonnie."

22

Phoebe snagged a cab heading inbound. She planned to pick up her Duster at the spot she'd been waylaid. She offered to drop me at home, but I decided to take the Muni instead. I caught the 38, transferred to the 22, and got off at Guerrero keeping an eye peeled for uniforms. The coast looked clear as I rounded onto Ramona, but I slipped quickly into the Toyota and sped away nonetheless.

I jerked to a halt just a few blocks away, across Market and up behind the Safeway. If somebody was watching my apartment, they seemed to have missed me sneaking off in the rental car. I took a long breath and let my heart get quiet. Then I rifled through the handful of tapes I'd stashed in the glove compartment. I pushed Lucinda Williams into the slot and played "Passionate Kisses" over and over for a spell of time. It's a habit of mine that drives people nuts. But when I'm hooked on a song, I can't seem to help it.

I was a big ball of sweat and grime, but I couldn't risk going home to take a shower. I rotated my sore shoulder and gave myself a pep talk. I gripped the wheel, noticing a swollen ridge across my right knuckles where I'd plowed my fist into

Monty's face. Finally, I stepped out of the car. It was too early to call on Jed Flack, so I made a beeline for the Mint in search of something wet and a glimpse of the evening news.

There was a stool with my name on it at the dark end of the bar. I hopped on and asked for a Bud. Barney was doing the honors tonight. He brought me a bottle and swatted the bar with a damp rag before setting it down. I peeled back a corner of the red and white label and said, "Anybody ask for me, Barney?"

"Why, honey? You lookin' for company?"

Barney was an enormous African-American man with a bald head and a tattoo of chain links that meandered from behind one ear down the length of his bicep. He also had a Pee Wee Herman voice and a wardrobe of XXXL sequined tank tops. It made for marvelous contrasts. I smiled.

"Nope. Matter of fact, I was hoping to remain anonymous just now."

"Fine by me, honey." Barney swiped at an imaginary spill. "You feel the tremors this morning?"

"No!"

Barney shook his head. "Biggest earthquake since last October. Series of 'em, actually. Everybody's all jazzed up about it." He gestured at the sprinkling of men gathered in noisy clusters throughout the Mint. "You must've been dead to the world."

I didn't much care for the allusion. I said, "What time was this, Barney?"

"Umm, about six, I guess. In the a.m."

"I'll be damned. Maybe there's some news about it." I pointed at the dusty Zenith perched on a ledge in the corner.

Barney said sure thing and reached up to click on the TV. I strained to hear the broadcast over the rattle and hum of jukebox melodies.

I got the gist of the earthquake news right away. Then a series of international reports—uprisings in Lithuania, tax revolts in Britain, escalated clashes in the Middle East. I swallowed some beer and started to feel miserable. Both for the traumas all over the world and for the smug complacency in the U.S. of A.

I was three-quarters into the bottle when the towheaded anchor came back with a local update. Police were investigating a fracas at the Cliff House today; two men were in stable condition, one with a gunshot wound to the thigh, the other a concussion. The police offered no other comments on the matter. That was it.

Either they hadn't yet connected the injured guys to Bellinski and Held—and to me, for that matter—or the cops were keeping it close to the cuff. In any event, it didn't tell me a thing, except that Armand Laws was going to pull through. I felt relieved. For Olive's sake, that is.

I ordered another Bud and honed in on the sportscast. The Cubs were humiliating the Giants in a series out at Candlestick. I smiled and wandered over to the pay phone. As usual, I couldn't reach Lydia Luchetti. Oh well. I left a message. My evening plans were shaping up to be pretty straightforward.

I lingered at the bar a bit longer, chatting with Barney and a friend of his named Julius who was now warming the seat beside me. Then I bid farewell and detoured to the bathroom to clean up. I was only semi-successful. I dabbed half-heartedly at my dirt-crusted knees and fastened the top button of my bowling shirt for that extra touch of sophistication. What the hell. I gave myself a little grin in the streaked mirror and headed out the door.

I decided to follow-up on one other notion before going to Flack's. Not such a straightforward evening after all. In musing on Cate Jones' whereabouts, I'd neglected to consider an obvious possibility—Club Femmes. The place seemed *too* conspicuous at first, but on further thought, it might be just the ticket. The club had been closed since Bellinski's death and stood vacant now, hanging in limbo, an urban shell waiting on a gang of high rollers.

I pointed the car toward Grove Street and fought a snarl of traffic jammed up near Davies Symphony Hall. Then I zigzagged over to Turk and felt a tire crunch over glass when I negotiated a tight parallel park. It was hopping down here, as usual. A group of women dressed to match the artwork that enlivened the front of Club Femmes was passing around something in a brown paper bag. Behind them, I could see the padlocked entrance to the club.

I slammed the car door and strolled over to the side alley. It was light enough in the early dusk to view the entire stretch. The metal door seemed flush with the building; bits of yellow police ribbon were still flapping around amidst all the other debris. I didn't see any humans back this way. I balled my fists in my pockets and walked quickly along the wall to check the side door. Yup, it was locked.

I hustled down to the end where a few cars hugged the back wall, and found that the alley veered to the right in an inverted L shape. I tucked around the corner. There was a rusty green dumpster back here, along with a sprinkling of used condoms that reminded me vaguely of a lawn of crushed cherry blossoms. Minus the aroma, of course.

I noticed a two-paned window cut in the cement wall at about chest level. It was too mud-caked to see inside, but when I reached up I discovered the frame was swinging loose from its upper hinge. I wondered if I could fit through. I stepped closer. Maybe if I could prop open the window.... I was rooting around on the ground for a stick when a flash of something white leaped out from among all the muck. It looked like a piece of cloth. I bent and poked it free from the dirt.

Good lord. It was the brown and white bordered handkerchief from Gillian Finer's apartment. That meant Olive Jones had been here today. Or that someone else had rifled my desk drawers and Olive had been telling me more lies.

I shoved the thing in my pocket and balanced in a crouch against the cold wall. A little arrhythmic hammering started up in my chest. I sprinted up to the dumpster. The rusty edges chafed my fingertips as I flipped back one side of the lid. A beery waft rose up from the soggy depths. I flexed my toes and peered over the rim. It was a nasty sight, but nothing you wouldn't expect from a downtown trash receptacle. Phew. I held my breath and reached inside for a jagged slat from a busted crate.

The piece of wood worked fine to keep the window ajar. It was a squeeze but I made it through and landed in a heap on a hard-packed dirt floor. A long trouser rip exposed my left leg from knee to ankle. I brushed myself off and adjusted my eyes to the dank interior. I appeared to be in some kind of storeroom; one wall was stacked with corrugated boxes, and a collection of beer kegs and empty bottles occupied another area. I passed through a corridor that led to the main room of Club Femmes. The only light I had with me was a tiny penlight attached to my keychain. I held it loosely in my right hand and began a systematic search of the premises.

I gave up after poking around for about an hour. I'd gained access to every room in the joint. Barring some subterranean hiding place, I was satisfied there was no one here. I deduced that people may have been here recently, though. The walk-in refrigerator lined with cases of beer also contained a supply of bread, luncheon meats, lettuce, and deli cartons of tuna fish and egg salad. All of it was still edible. And not the kind of stuff you'd serve up as bar nibbles to the sweaty habitués of a topless dance hall.

The cops had thoroughly ransacked Bellinski's office, but I found one item of note. Underneath the cushion of the Naugahyde chair, a miniature key was nestled among a smattering of change. It looked just like a handcuff key. I palmed it, along with seventy-three cents. I also checked through Bellinski's desk, but anything of relevance—like financial records or phone bills or an address book—had apparently been removed.

I retraced my steps and ripped a few more slits in my clothing on my way out of the Club Femmes. The light was fading fast. A couple of young men were hunkered down on the far side of the dumpster, but if they noticed me slithering out of the building it didn't faze them at all. I jogged around the L and out to the mouth of the alley. Then I crossed the street, fired up the Toyota, and played "Passionate Kisses" one more time.

23

It was easy to park in Jed Flack's neighborhood
early on a Saturday night. On this slope of
Potrero Hill, everybody must be out tasting
sun-dried tomatoes and pepper vodka at some
far-flung eatery. From my vantage point at the
crest of Missouri at 22nd Street, I could see blackish bay waters
glimmering in the remnants of evening light. Stepping out of
the driver's seat, I also caught the view down the backside of
the hill: neglected housing developments, junked out autos,
and stretches of vacant land where now-defunct railroad and
shipping companies used to be headquartered. They could run
urban field trips out in this neighborhood to illustrate the
growing chasm between rich and poor.

A group of kids tossed a football around in a park on my
left, making unnervingly gleeful noises as they took turns
pummeling each other into the ground. I turned onto Flack's
street, scanning the numbers.

Almost every house on the block had undergone recent
renovations; fresh pastel paint jobs shone from a number of
the Victorians, and modernized decks and landscaped terraces
were in evidence, too. Flack lived about halfway down on the

left in a pointy triple-decker in soft gray tones with dusty red trim. I spied his name printed boldly on the mailbox and contemplated the one light I saw illuminating a ground floor room.

I wasn't fearful of Flack himself. He seemed the type to hire out his dirty work. But I didn't know if I could get him to come clean. Even if I threatened to expose my suspicions of his hypocritical business dealings, I had nothing concrete to pin him to Bellinski, Held, and the Joneses. I might just get a door slammed in my face for all my efforts.

Still, he was my best chance right now to sew up some loose ends and get a new lead on Cate Jones. Judging from the desperate behavior of Monty and Armand, Jed Flack might well be scrambling now, too, and be easy prey for a pushy p.i.

I glanced down at my disheveled attire, made a few fruitless adjustments. Oh well. I squared my shoulders and strolled up the walk. When I punched the bell, a sound of tinkling piano keys halted abruptly. Nothing happened for a minute or two. I hit the doorbell again.

Then I heard a padding of footsteps from within. A porch light pinned me to the stoop and I saw some motion behind the glassy peephole. Somebody let the door crack a few inches, as far as the safety chain would allow.

"Yes?" a raspy voice said.

"Hello," I said in a sunshiny chirp. "Is Jed in?"

One sea-green eye peered through the crack. "What do you want?"

"To speak with Jed. We're involved in a, ah...an enterprise together and I need to clear some things up." I paused. "It's urgent."

The door closed. Then opened again. "Who are you?"

What the hell. "Nell Fury."

It must have meant something to Mr. Raspy. The door came fully open this time to reveal a polished tile hallway lined on one side with a gilt-edged mirror. The man reflected there was a cuddly sort in a pale pink cardigan, gray designer sweats, and a ragtop of sandy brown hair. Whoever he was, he wasn't Jed Flack. I took in his whiskbroom moustache and wracked my brain—I knew I'd seen him somewhere before.

He stubbed out his cigarette in an ashtray on a low table and reached up to gesture me inside. There was a deep worry line between his eyes of more recent vintage than his two matching arcs of crow's feet. He looked me over quizzically, then shrugged and said, "Jed's not home right now but... come on in."

Click. It was the guy from the *Examiner* society page. In the photo with Flack and his ex-wife. The new husband, what was his name...Novacek! Aha. William Novacek.

He shuffled his slippered feet and nodded me into an adjacent room. A lacquered upright piano was the key feature, along with a couple of new-ish couches that might have come from Pier 1. We both kept standing.

"Miss Fury..."

"Nell."

"—Nell, Jed's out of town. I'm a...family friend. Name's Willy."

I nodded. "I know he's in Nevada. Do you expect him home soon?"

"I don't know, I'm just—" He reddened. "How did you know where he was? What are you doing here?!"

I reached for my supply of business cards and handed one to Novacek. He took a quick glance then curled it in his spidery fingers. He was caught in a silent struggle—whether to kick me out or whether to confide in me. I said, "Willy, we both know more than we're letting on. You recognized my name, right?"

He sunk into one of the couches. "Yeah. From the news report of that guy...getting murdered. Jed introduced me to him once at a party. Then Jed left town after he got shot. I knew he was going to Reno like he often does, but this was different, like—"

I waited. "Like?"

"—like something was wrong."

"You think he was involved in Bellinski's murder?"

Willy Novacek pulled the sleeves of his sweater down over his knuckles and started fussing with the wool. "No! No, of course not. But...I think he's in trouble." He fixed me with his watery eyes, then suddenly shook himself up from the

137

couch. He cast a guarded glance at my muddied attire, then went on, "Here, sit down. Let me get you something."

I shrugged. "Just water, please. No ice."

Willy returned a minute later with two tumblers of H_2O. It looked as if he'd tried to compose himself in the kitchen, but he still seemed afraid. In more ways than one. I decided to clear up part of the problem.

"You live here, don't you Willy?"

"No, I'm a friend, I—" He faltered.

"I know. You're married to Jed's ex."

"Yes, how—" This time his flush almost matched his cardigan. He fumbled in his pocket for a pack of Exports, the kind in the gold box.

I said: "I saw a photo in the paper. Of the three of you. It used to be called 'bearding.'"

A throaty laugh came out of his mouth. "It still is."

I smiled back. "I know. So what's the point? You can hang out with Jed without rousing suspicion, he looks like a sensitive man for staying close to his ex-wife. What does Nadine get out of it?"

"Oh, Nadine." Willy let out a shroud of smoke. "She's kind of ambitious. I guess she likes the influence, you know, the sparkle of knowing a politician. She's always networking. She and Jed don't have much in common any more but she still gets to meet lots of people through him."

"What does she do?"

Willy waved a hand. "Umm, business. Trading, that kind of thing."

I let it go for now. "And how long have you and Jed been together?"

"God. Eleven years. Jed's okay—" There went that blush. "—I mean, he's great. He cares about this city, you know, he works real hard. I think he should come out of the closet, already. It's not like people don't know."

"So...?"

"He's waiting for his dad to die. Thinks the old man would keel over if he found out." We both guffawed at the irony. I leaned back and took a sip of water, then rested my bruised knuckles against the cool outside of the glass.

"So you said Jed's in Reno. What does he do there, visit his father?"

"Yeah, except—" Willy cast down his eyes, then distracted himself with a hunt for an ashtray. He found one and squished out the Export. "Nell, look, like I said, I think Jed's in trouble. But I don't know...he said he'd be back tonight—"

"What—did he go someplace else? Do you know what he was up to?"

"No!" Willy Novacek was unable to muster any anger. He just seemed scared. Sighing, he explained, "Jed said he might go down south after he went to Reno. He had to see somebody in Beatty."

"Where's that? Near Las Vegas?"

"Uh huh, thereabouts. In Nye County. I don't know what he was doing there, though. Christ, I wish I did."

I remembered what Emily Winkmeyer had told me about prostitution in Nevada. How influence peddling might be a little easier on the outskirts of Vegas, far from the shadow of the Mustang Ranch. But I wondered if the Flack name would carry any clout down there. "Willy," I said slowly, "did Jed ever mention anything about starting a business in Nevada? Say with his father, or anybody?"

"No." Novacek was on his feet again, tugging at the distended sleeves of his cardigan.

"Why do you think he's in trouble?"

Novacek just looked at me with blank round eyes.

I decided to bone him up on what I thought was going on. I figured he'd be an ally, worried as he was. I launched into a partial explanation, half-expecting Flack to come traipsing in at any moment.

"...I'm not saying Jed had anything to do with Cate's disappearance. I think Bellinski did, though, and if he and Jed were working together—" I shrugged. "Plus, Gillian Finer's unaccounted for. And I saw her with Jed. They could be up to something."

"I met her once," Willy said. "Bright red hair, right? Kind of...affected?"

I turned up my lips. "That's her."

Willy was back on the couch. A calico cat had appeared and glued itself to his thigh. He stroked the purring mound nervously. "I can't believe Jed would be involved with that kind of...prostitution thing. He's a feminist, a liberal—"

I interrupted with an inadvertent staccato chuckle. "Willy, liberals are the chief proponents of the sex industry these days. Free speech and all. The First Amendment." I wondered if I sounded hopelessly cynical.

"So you think Jed's been using his connections back home to help Bellinski and this guy Lockenwood open a whorehouse?"

"I think it's a possibility. Maybe he's using his connections here, too. For other ventures in the city."

"But why would—" Novacek lowered his eyelids.

"Do you know much about Nadine's investments?"

He kept his eyes glued and shook his head. I was depressing Willy in a big way. Just one more twist of the knife. I told him about Nadine's stake in Boom Properties' plan to build a hotel and convention site in the Tenderloin. And suggested that Jed might be getting a cut of the action. In fact, perhaps Bellinski offered Boom a good deal on the Club Femmes property in exchange for Jed's help in Nevada.

"Oh, this is too much," Willy said. "This is crazy. You have no proof! Jed's not...no."

I was still clutching my empty water glass. I set it on an end table and leaned forward, suddenly dazed with weariness. I said, "Look, it *is* crazy. But Bellinski's dead, Lockenwood's frantic, Finer's laying low..." I shrugged. "I know Cate Jones is still missing. Either Jed had something to do with it or he's in danger, too."

Willy Novacek jumped up, thumping the cat onto the floor. "Maybe I should call Nadine."

He didn't move so I said, "Does Jed stay with his father when he goes to Reno?"

"Yeah. Or sometimes he goes to the cabin."

"Where's that?"

"At Tahoe. On the Nevada side, near Stateline. It's an old family place of Jed's."

"Does Nadine ever stay there?"

"Sure. It's empty a lot of times. But yeah, we all go there."

I got him to give me directions to the cabin, coaxing all the while. I didn't begrudge him his reluctance. I was skeptical of all this hunch-playing myself. By the time I mobilized to take my leave, Jed Flack had still not returned home. Nor had Willy put in a call to his "wife," Nadine Flack Novacek. I left him polishing a long double track in the hallway tile with the soles of his J. Crew suede slippers.

I retrieved the car and positioned it at the end of the street, pointed so I could see Flack's front door. It was tranquil in the hilltop neighborhood, except for occasional blasts from a stereo and the distant whir of wheels on the highway. I sat there till my watch read 1:45 a.m. in the amber glow of the street light. Then I cranked the ignition and pulled away, head foggy with sleepiness and worry.

24

It was a gutsy move, all things considered, but I was feeling low on options. I didn't dare go home yet; I wanted to avoid an encounter with the badges until I'd untangled this imbroglio or exhausted all hope. I thought about going to Phoebe's, but that was such an obvious place to look for me. Besides, Phoebe was probably occupied.

And Tad was out of the question. Don't ask me why.

So I dropped two bits in a pay phone on Folsom Street and called Tammie Rae Tinkers.

She came on after four rings. "Hmmph?"

"Rae? Sorry Rae, it's me, Nell."

"Nell. Hello." Her voice sounded like a rumble of storm clouds in the wake of a summer shower. It took me a moment to respond.

"Hi Rae. Did I wake you?"

Throaty laughter. "Um-hm. Ummm. I tried to call you today."

"Well, ha ha, here I am." Wow, this woman made me nervous. "I had a, uh, rough day."

"Is everything okay?"

"Oh yeah. Now it is. Except—" I picked at the edge of a *Silencio=Muerte* sticker that was plastered to the base of the phone. "I need a place to stay."

"Sure. Oh—" Rae stopped. "You mean right now?"

"Uh huh."

"Oh. Okay, well come on. You remember where I live?"

"Yeah. Number 250, right?"

"Yup." Rae made a soft noise. "Are you close by?"

"In the Mission."

"See you soon then."

"Bye," I said.

"Bye."

I'd been to Rae's apartment once before, for an impromptu brunch out on her fire escape. We'd mixed brandy in with the orange juice and watched cars flow like regimented space mobiles up the concrete on-ramp to Highway 101. She lived toward the eastern end of Page Street, midway between the Zen Center on one corner and a crowd of street corner worshippers on the next block who pushed a different sort of salvation altogether. It was a nice place. I liked the city views from her broad window and the one-room practicality of the apartment, complete with its black iron-framed Murphy bed.

Rae buzzed me in and I climbed to the second floor. She was waiting for me at the end of the hall wearing a wide-waled corduroy robe faded the color of whole wheat toast. She offered me a genteel peck and ushered me inside, chain-locking the door behind us.

I sat on the corner of the bed and smoothed my palms over the thighs of my crusted khakis.

Rae blinked. "You're a mess, Nell."

I gave her a little half-hearted grin. I didn't feel like talking about it.

"Well." She came and sat close to me, one leg tucked into the folds of her robe. It was an old-fashioned garment buttoned clear up to her neck. I noticed tiny crinkles around the outsides of her eyes and a crease mark along her cheek that might have come from a pillow. Rae said, "Can I get you anything?"

"No but...do you mind if I take a shower?"

She smiled and shook her head no.

I lingered in the stream of water for awhile, clenching and unclenching my sore right hand. The rest of me felt okay, energetic almost. I scoped out Rae's selection of shampoos—there were half a dozen varieties lining an alcove on the back wall of the shower. I settled on something thick and brown that smelled like redwood trees. When I finished, I surveyed my tattered clothes, shrugged, and wrapped myself up in a big peach bath towel.

Rae had turned out all the lights except for a small bedside lamp that cast an egg-shaped shadow against the wall. She was reading one of the books she'd borrowed from my Favorite Lesbian Novels collection, Denise Ohio's *The Finer Grain*. She stuck a finger between the pages and rolled over to welcome me. The corduroy robe was in a pile on the floor and Rae wore nothing but a cream-colored lace camisole. I walked over and lay down full on top of her.

The book skittered to the floor as Rae met me with a big open-mouthed kiss. She tasted like salt and toothpaste and something hard to pinpoint, and all those weeks of desire for her came welling forward and caught me in a chokehold. It was hard to breathe for a minute, but I didn't care, and we stayed mashed together for a countless bit of time. Then she made a sound and said, "Nell, can you take off the towel? It's really wet."

I flipped sideways and peeled away the soggy terry cloth. Rae was gazing down the length of my body and I shivered, feeling a rivulet of moisture fall from a lock of my hair and land in the hollow between my breasts. Rae licked it off.

"You're kind of wet now, too," I said, playfully teasing down the strap of her top.

She beamed at me and twisted back, giving me plenty of room to maneuver. I took my time pulling the camisole over her head, letting my hands trail up her sides and across the tips of her nipples. When I was done I kissed her again, all around the side of her neck and along the back of her hairline.

She fell onto the sheets and I pressed against her from behind. Rae reached around and ran her thumb up the inside of my thigh. I must have made some noise because Rae chuckled deep in her throat and rolled over again, resting her right palm along the crest of my hipbone. I drew up a knee to separate her legs and she gasped a little. It turned into a laugh and I couldn't help it, I was cracking up, too, and we lay there kissing and laughing and feeling each other up all over. Everything seemed funny to me all of a sudden, like it sometimes does during sex. In this case, it was a good kind of funny.

Rae was having her period and we talked about that for awhile. Then I explained for the millionth time that I have herpes, but it's okay, I know when I have sores. And I didn't have one right now. Rae smiled. I reached up to entwine my fingers in her hair and I felt a painful fullness in my chest, as if I might start weeping. It all seemed so serious again. Rae's eyes were almost violet against the opaque black of her pupils. I took a big gulp of air and then we proceeded, Rae's hand meandering down to stroke the inside of my soaked labia.

We sweated the bed up pretty thoroughly before the night was out, and I went through a thousand more cycles of shyness and amusement. As I was falling asleep, Rae tucked behind me in a spoon, she asked, "What is it you like about being a private eye?"

"Ummmm. You get to meet beautiful women and bed down with them."

"Hmmph." I was beginning to love that little half-laugh, half-guffaw of Rae's. She drawled, "I get to do that in my profession, too."

"You do? What field did you say you were in? Maybe there's an opening for me."

"Left field, honey, same as you." Rae nipped into my shoulder blade.

"Ahhh," I said. "I like that."

My hair had dried into a capful of matted curls. Rae tugged gently at one frizzed hunk and whispered, "Really, Nell, why do you do it?"

I rolled onto my back and looked up into the shadows. Rae had affixed a glow-in-the-dark stencil set to the ceiling. Winking down at us was a seemingly random array of stars and half-moons, cut out with cartoonish clarity like the marshmallow chunks in Lucky Charms cereal. Rae probably couldn't tell I was smiling.

I leaned over and kissed her on the forehead. "I can't answer that right now, Rae. Why don't you ask me again in the morning?"

She said okay and we nestled together once more. I knew that even if she remembered to bring it up again, I still wouldn't have a ready answer.

25

I had wanted to get up early, but I realized I'd overslept when I woke to a stream of brilliant daylight coursing through the window. The apartment smelled of coffee. I lay still for a moment and listened to Rae moving around in the bathroom. She emerged wearing a short navy blue jumper over a sheer sleeveless blouse. Her feet were bare and she had resculpted her spit curls into two perfect loops. What a knockout. She paused in midstep when she saw I was awake.

"Hello. Want some coffee?"

"In a minute." I messed up Rae's hairdo a bit before wending my way to the bathroom. I washed up and eyeballed my crumpled pants and shirt. Then I went to find Rae to see if she had anything I could borrow. She fished out a pair of worn-thin Levi 501s that were loose in just the right places, and an old white T-shirt with a tiny "Loveless Motel" emblem over one breast. She explained it was a joint outside of Nashville—its cafe was famous for country ham and gravy, eggs, grits, and biscuits. That gave us some ideas, so we settled at her kitchen counter over a slightly less ambitious breakfast. In addition to all her other ace qualities, Tammie Rae Tinkers made a mean cup of joe.

I didn't get out of there until almost 11:30 a.m. Rae walked me down to the intersection of Market and Laguna; I'd left the car nearby and she intended to pick up a Sunday paper at the corner store. We engaged in some flashy public display in lieu of your everyday goodbye. Then I watched her walk all the way into the store before I turned, sighed, and aimed for the public phone at the laundromat. I wanted to try Lydia Luchetti one more time.

I'd called her from Rae's about an hour before, to no avail. I was planning to drive to Lake Tahoe today, but I really hoped to chat with Luchetti before hitting the road. If I still couldn't reach her, maybe I'd check in with Tad Greenblatt. I punched Luchetti's number. Listening to the rings, I wondered how things had gone with Phoebe and Johnnie Blue last night. Then I remembered Flannery and Carson—did they have enough grub?

Luchetti picked up, her voice coming over the wire in a hoarse rush. "Yeah?"

"Hi Lydia, it's Nell Fury."

"Nell! Fuck—where have you been? I've called your machine about fifty times."

"Oh, I—"

"Never mind. Listen, they got Olive Jones."

"What?!" I stared at a lime green blur clogging up the viewing window of the clothes dryer in front of me. "What do you mean? Who's 'they?'"

"The cops."

"How did they find her?" My mind was racing ahead, contemplating the ins and outs of this new development.

"Who knows, they're cops. When Meg was down there..." Luchetti explained that she heard about the arrest through her lover Margaret Halliway, District Attorney for the City and County of San Francisco. Luchetti was privy to a lot of information that way, and I was one of few confidantes who knew that Halliway and Luchetti were an item. It made me weary to keep track of piteous secrets like that. But it was nice to have an indirect pipeline to the office of the highest prosecutor in town.

I listened while Luchetti told me they had booked Olive Jones for Godfrey Bellinski's murder, and for the attempt on

Armand Laws. They were hoping to tag her for Melvin Held, too. She also said the police were steaming mad at me.

I sighed. "Was there any mention of Jed Flack throughout all of this?"

"No," Luchetti said, "they're just calling it a revenge type of thing. A jealousy motive in the case of Bellinski's murder. I don't think they know what to make of you and Armand Laws and those other people—"

Good. They didn't seem to know it was Phoebe I'd been with at the Cliff House.

"—and the injured guys, Monty whatever-his-name-is and Laws, they're not talking. What happened out at—"

I knew she was revving up to probe me about the Cliff House incident. I cut her off. "Forget it, Lydia. Did you get anywhere on the Flack thing?"

"Shit." She sounded pissed. "No, not really. Except I found out Flack hired a private eye to find out what *you* know. So something must be up."

"Yeah, I know about that." Gee, so much for *private* investigating. E-Z was such a simple outfit to crack, it veered more on the public than private.

Luchetti said: "Umm. I found out some info on Nadine Novacek, too. Now there's a sleazy operator."

The green swirl of laundry faltered and collapsed as the dryer clicked to a halt. A woman in a shroud of plastic pink hair rollers came over and poked around, but the load must have still been wet because she let out an expletive and threw in more quarters. I asked Lydia what she'd learned about Nadine.

"She exercises a lot of power in real estate circles, and—through Jed Flack—among politicians, too. She's been influential in a couple of big zoning decisions, like the changes in the Tenderloin that have cleared the way for recent development. And she puts up money to fight any rent control initiative. Plus, she works with a couple of those high-priced union-busting consultants. That's about it. She's careful to keep it all legal, at least it seems that way..."

"Hmmm, and if she and Jed are still chummy..." I trailed off without mentioning I had met Willy Novacek.

"So Flack's a hypocrite," Luchetti said, "no way around it."

"But is that all there is to it?"

"Right. That's what I want to know..." Luchetti badgered me with some more questions, which I sidestepped impatiently. Now I was really eager to see what was going on at the lakeside cabin in Nevada. But first I asked, "Does Olive Jones have an attorney?"

"Sure. But she blabbed for awhile before some do-gooder cop warned her to keep it zipped until her lawyer arrived. Meg said she kept mentioning 'home'—I guess Olive was talking to somebody at the motel about her home when the police showed up. They thought she was talking nonsense. They didn't pay attention and she finally shut up."

"They didn't ask...shit!"

"What?"

"Who was she talking to at the motel?"

"A desk clerk, I think. Why?"

"A man? A woman? What?"

"I don't know—no, it was a guy. Somebody just in for the morning shift. He didn't know what was going on. Why?"

"Do you know the guy's name?"

"No. Nell! What's going on?"

"Lydia, I doubt she was talking about home just because of a sudden burst of nostalgia. I gotta go." I hung up to the sounds of her protestations. I suppose I owed Luchetti a scoop, but I wouldn't even have one to pass along if I stood around schmoozing much longer.

The Toyota was parked at a meter on Market Street. Lucky for me, the metermaids give it a rest on Sunday. I slid onto the plush red seat, which was toasting slowly in the hot midday sun. I quickly cranked a window and rolled up my T-shirt sleeves, sorry again not to have my sunglasses. I merged into the sparse traffic heading outbound and hung a few turns through the maze of Duboce Triangle. Then I headed north on Divisadero and rode the hills until the final downhill stretch sent me shooting forward with a spectacular panoramic view that spread out clear across the Bay from Yerba Buena Island to Alcatraz to the hills of Sausalito, and over the treetops of the Presidio to the Golden Gate Bridge and beyond.

I turned right onto Lombard Street. It was a little less scenic down this way. I'd found the name of Olive Jones' motel on the matchbook I'd transferred—along with all my other junk—from one pants pocket to another. The Cow Hollow Motor Inn was a prefab kind of place that fit in well with its neighboring establishments on this commercial slice of Lombard. I left the car in a loading zone around the corner on Steiner and hustled back to the lobby of the inn.

It was a bustling place on a Sunday, little clumps of tourists waiting to check out, or maybe check in, or get their cars fetched, or have their suitcases toted from one spot to another. In fact, it was a hapless looking crowd overall, except for the employees in tan uniforms with red militaristic piping who darted around taking care of people's needs. I waylaid one fellow who was expressing his individuality with a pair of silver noserings that threaded through one pasty nostril and clashed with the gold buttons of his uniform.

"Excuse me, do you know who was working the front desk this morning?"

"Heyyyy. I been to the Loveless." He gave me a complete once-over and settled his focus back on my left breast. I wondered what would happen if I tugged really hard on the noserings.

"Is that a fact," I said flatly. "So about the desk clerk—"

"Yessss ma'am, quite a place. Quite a place. You from Tennessee?" He was leaning in real close with that let's-be-friends kind of body language.

I took a step back. "Yup. Me and Dolly, we're like this." I held up two crossed fingers and wagged them in his face, then wheeled around in search of another tan uniform.

An older guy with Coke bottle glasses and a kinder, gentler smile pointed me toward a door that opened into a corridor near the front desk. He said Richie was back there in the employee's lounge, first room on the left. I strode through the hall and rapped on the closed door. Somebody called out "Yo!" so I twisted the knob and stepped into the drab room. A few workers were shooting the breeze over vending machine coffee and a box of donuts.

"Yeah?" a woman asked.

"I'm looking for Richie."

A man with his feet propped on the table set down a powdered sugar donut and looked at me blankly. He was Asian, younger than me, annoyed at being disturbed on his break. He ran the back of his hand over his powdery lips and said, "What?"

"Can I speak with you for a minute, please?"

"I already talked to the cops."

"I'm not with the police. I—" I fidgeted. "It'll just take a minute."

Richie dropped his feet to the floor with a clunk, then shrugged and followed me out to the hallway. Chatter resumed behind us and I pulled the door closed. I thought a show of legitimacy might help, so I dug a business card out of my pocket. This batch was getting rather mangled. When Richie looked over the card, a tiny prick of curiosity seemed to light up in his eyes. "What's up?" he intoned.

"Thanks for talking to me, Richie. I understand you were working the front desk this morning when Olive Jones got arrested."

"Yup."

"I heard you were in the middle of a conversation with her when the cops arrived, something about her home..."

Richie crossed his arms. "Yeah. So what? It was no big deal."

"Well, the way I heard it, she was kind of agitated about something." I raised my eyebrows.

"Uh huh. She missed a phone call. I was giving her the message, that's all, and—" He frowned. "—yeah, she got a little tweaked. Then a bunch of squad cars pulled up and that was the end of that."

"Can you tell me what the phone message was, please?"

Richie took another look at my business card. Then he hunched his shoulders and said with a touch of exasperation, "Somebody named Kate called, said to leave a message for the woman in Room 65—Olive Jones. To tell her to come home. That she was there and Olive should come home, too."

"And Olive got upset when you gave her the message?"

"Yup. She kept asking me for more details, cursing that she'd missed the call, pressing me. Man, that's all I knew!"

I thought for a moment. "Richie, did the cops pay any attention to what Olive Jones was saying?"

"Uh uh. They read her those rights..." He shook his head, as if suddenly aware of the drama he'd been in the midst of. "Then they carted her off. Murder...shit."

I thanked him and crossed through the lobby to a bank of pay phones I'd noticed on the way in. It looked like I'd be rerouting my travel plans for the day. Just in case Cate—or Cate's imposter—had been referring to the lower Twin Peaks apartment as "home," I dialed Gillian Finer's number. No answer. No surprise. Next I tried the Jones' house in Pacific Palisades. No answer there, either, but curiously, the phone machine failed to come on. I pushed a handful of change back into the slot and punched one more L.A. number.

"Hullllo?"

"Martha? Hi, it's Marcia Rhodes."

"Oh, Marcia, my dear, how are you?"

Wow. It's like we were fast friends. "Fine, thanks," I said. "You know, I still haven't been in touch with Olive or Cate. Have you seen them around their house?"

"No!" Martha made a couple of tsk, tsk noises. "Those policemen aren't around anymore, thank goodness. They made such a fuss whenever I went to feed the puppy."

"Did they ever tell you what was going on?" I asked trepidatiously.

"No sirree! And I haven't seen them now since yesterday afternoon. Dear me. Do *you* know what's going on?"

"No," I said too quickly. "Well, so no one's been at the house you say?"

"Noooo. But there's a car parked down the street, right outside my house, as a matter of fact, that looks like something Cate would drive. She always had rather, uhhh, flashy taste. It's a real clean, shiny white car. So I thought maybe Cate was home visiting, you know? But she wasn't there when I went in and—"

A shiny white car. Hmm. Martha rattled on while I ran that image around in my brain and tried to remember its significance. A white car...whoa...a white Camaro had been parked in Bellinski's driveway the first time I'd gone snooping in Orinda. So it was either Cate's...or it belonged to somebody who knew Cate and had business in both locations.

I butted in on Martha. "Is that car a Camaro?"

"Um, a Camaro. Yes, I suppose it is."

"Listen, I have to go now. You be careful around the Jones house, okay?" She couldn't possibly know what I meant, and I didn't elaborate. I rang off to the sounds of "my dear..." and rehooked the receiver. My decision was clinched.

The Toyota was a veritable sauna by the time I climbed back in. I fired her up and was on the road again.

26

It was 7:10 p.m. by my watch when I turned onto the Pacific Coast Highway. I'd made decent time to Los Angeles, stopping only once to refuel and pick up a package of Fig Newtons. Now I retraced my route alongside the ocean and into the canyons at the base of the Santa Monica Mountains. Pacific Palisades was as tony and secluded as ever, but I felt a clamoring anxiousness in my gut as I neared the turn-off to Toyopa Drive.

I needed a toilet; I figured I'd better improvise. I pulled onto a gravel shoulder and traipsed down a small incline that led me through tangled bramble and around a rocky ledge. The Pacific opened out in front of me, lapping at a jagged beach. A series of modest cottages sprinkled the pale sand like blacked-out spaces on a crossword puzzle. I dropped my pants and thought about the task in front of me.

I strongly believed Cate Jones was at the Pacific Palisades home. Whether by choice or under coercion, I still didn't know. I also expected to find Jed Flack there, and possibly Gillian Finer. The trick would be to disrupt their operation while insuring Cate's welfare—that is, if it needed insuring.

First I planned to scope out the situation myself. If it looked too hairy, I'd call on the L.A. uniforms.

I realized Darnelle Comey's nifty pick locks were back at my apartment. Damn. I also didn't have any toilet paper or tissues. I wasn't living up to my scouting pledge, "Be Prepared." Then I remembered the handkerchief I'd retrieved from the dirt outside Club Femmes. I drew it out of a back pocket, flapped it in the breeze, and made do with the soiled square. It brought a whole new meaning to the notion of tampering with the evidence.

I buttoned my fly and scooted back to the Toyota, pondering one sticky point. If I successfully defused the situation down here, would I feel comfortable relating the entire saga to the San Francisco Police? I guess I had no choice, unless Phoebe was really ready to move on our "Bonnie and Bonnie" plan. But I wondered what the cops had to lose in this whole affair...hmm. They seemed so eager to simply throw the book at Olive Jones.

Then there was the matter of Mean Joe Lockenwood.

I mulled over these concerns while I drove the last couple of miles to the Jones' street. The sky was a big, broad wash of blue-gray with a cloud cover blocking out the sunset. A few slivers of orange poked through, though, and I kept the car lights off as I cruised along Toyopa and checked out the front view at #437.

Everything appeared closed up and sedate. I rolled past and around a corner; there was the white vehicle Martha had mentioned. It was a Camaro alright, and although I couldn't be sure, I thought it was the same car I'd seen in the Orinda driveway. I noted the license plate number this time and stopped the Toyota a few hundred more feet up the road.

There were some solos and couples out dog-walking in the neighborhood—a popular local pastime, it seemed. But nobody paid me as much mind as Martha had. Fortunately, I didn't bump into her. I walked briskly back toward the Jones' house and slunk into a patch of trees off to one side. I stayed there about fifteen minutes, and failed to see any movement or lights go on or off within the house. In the deepening dusk, the metal sculptures on the lawn glinted with the sinister menace of a collection of medieval torture devices.

If I had the pick locks, I'd approach from the back. Since I didn't, I was hoping the key was still situated above the front door frame. I strode over and reached up a confident hand. Hooray. There was no one in sight as I unlocked the door and slipped noiselessly inside. Then I dug the security code out of my memory—correctly, I hoped—and hit a series of numbers on the rectangular panel.

It seemed to do the trick, or perhaps the system wasn't even on. Whatever. I stood there a moment letting my heart rate settle and my eyes get accustomed to the interior gloom.

A bit of light was flickering at the end of the hall on the left. The kitchen was back that way, and as I crept along the length of the corridor I heard a soft patter of voices. A couple of women were conversing. I couldn't see them from where I was, but judging from the clink of glassware and the way the light was jumping erratically against one wall, they were in the middle of a candlelight supper. How quaint.

I came to an alcove near the end of the hall that was half-obscured by a hinged rice paper door. It looked like some kind of pantry. There was just enough space to squeeze inside. I ducked through the opening and positioned myself flat against the wall, careful to avoid knocking anything off the neatly ordered shelves. I listened.

"...did you get enough shrimp?"

"Yeah, thanks. Can you pass the wine, though?"

"Ummm."

I heard a splash. Silence. Then a big sigh.

"So after we...do it, we're just supposed to leave the bodies here?"

"Yeah. I finally touched base with Joe. He's going to send somebody around tomorrow, burn this place down."

"God."

"Oh, Gillian, you're so sentimental." She sighed. "Nobody can tie this to us. Monty and Armand—they'll be too cowed to talk. You know, it's a good thing Olive got arrested. They'll stick her with the murders and—"

I heard a slurp as she paused, mid-sentence.

"—the blaze, it'll go down as an accident."

"But what about the inheritance? This is so fucked up—"

The other woman cut in; there was a hint of irritation in her voice. "Forget about it! Sure, maybe you won't get Cate's money. Olive'll get some shyster to contest the damn will. But you never know, it might still work. You could make it a test case for the validity of domestic partnerships." She laughed.

Gillian Finer swore.

Her dinner partner said, "Gilly, hey. Considering what's happened, things are working out. I'll make a bundle through Boom Properties. I've got *lots* of new investment ideas. And Joe's a creative kind of guy; he'll find somebody else to front money for the whorehouse. We'll all get a cut of that, and with Jed in there influencing zoning decisions—"

"He's starting to get suspicious, Nadine."

Nadine.

"So what? What's Jed going to do? He can't bag out now, not after pulling all those strings in Nye County, not after going in on the hotel."

"This sucks!" A chair screeched against the floor, then something broke with a splintering crash. I couldn't tell if Gillian had knocked over a glass, or if one of them had hurled it on purpose.

Nadine cursed. "What the hell are you doing? What, *now* you're getting cold feet? Fucking princess."

"Don't yell at me!" Gillian's voice cracked, caught midway between anger and misery. I heard a rhythmic tread, as if she'd started pacing the kitchen. "I don't know, I don't want—"

Nadine butted in. "What's that?"

"What?!"

"I thought I heard something."

Damn. Olive Jones' little dog was clattering down the hallway. It stopped to sniff around a few feet shy of the pantry.

Gillian was crying. She uttered, "I think it's just the dog."

"Go check it out."

Her footsteps changed course and headed in my direction. I could see the shock of her dayglow hair through the slats in the rice paper. I held my breath.

"It's just the stupid mutt," she said.

"No! Go make sure they're not up to something." Geez, that Nadine Novacek sure was the demanding sort. Gillian seemed to regain her edge. She said, "Fuck!" and walked off toward another part of the house.

I released some air. The dog loped into the pantry and started lapping at my shoes. I lifted a foot and tried to nudge it gently away. It just kept licking.

Gillian came back. "They're right where we left them."

"Okay. Gilly, I'm sorry. But you can't, I mean...the ball's rolling. We're in this now, together. Okay?"

"Yeah."

A chair scraped again and I heard more sounds of rattling forks. Gillian was still riled up. She suddenly burst out, "If I get that money, I'm not giving any to Lockenwood! He promised this was a flawless plan, he said—"

"No. You'd be crazy to cross him."

"I hate it—these guys running everything! I could've pulled off this job without dragging those stupid assholes into it—"

Nadine tried to soothe her. "I know, I know. But it takes time to establish a reputation, you know, to get some power. You can't mess around with Lockenwood. Just stick with me, it's going to get better for us..."

The dog started in with some tiny yammering noises. I was afraid old Spot would blow my cover. I needed to get out of there. Besides, it was time to make a move to free the captives. As I tiptoed out of the closet, I heard Nadine say, "...finish up, let's get it over with..."

I slid along the hallway away from the jiggling candlelight. When I rounded a corner to head in the direction of the bathroom, the corridor was shrouded in darkness. I felt my way along the wall. My shoe made a tapping sound as I stepped over a threshold at the far end of the hall. I stopped. Nothing. I wiped my palms on my jeans and waited a few more beats.

I still couldn't hear anything. So I dug out my penlight and—keeping it pointed to the ground—quickly searched the rooms at this side of the house. I was heading into the last room on the right when a raspy breathing from within broke the stillness. I flicked off my light and moved softly through the doorway. Two figures were slumped in a corner. Through the murky shadows I could tell that one was prone to the floor and the other slouched against a chair with arms pinned back. I flashed my light on again.

One of the people squeaked.

"Sshhh!" I trotted forward with a finger to my lips. The woman on the floor wasn't moving. Although I could only see part of her face, I knew right away it was Cate Jones. There was that same jawline, the lanky bone structure. She was wearing plain black pants and a white button-down shirt, and both appeared disheveled and stained. A smell of urine and stale sweat emanated from the corner.

Then I glanced at the upright figure beside her. Jesus Christ. Darnelle Comey of E-Z Investigative Services was gaping at me with her big pea soup eyes. I felt a very untimely urge to laugh. I stifled it. Kneeling beside her I whispered, "So Darnelle, you're getting quite a first-hand look at criminalistics, aren't you?"

"Oh, Ms. Fury..."

I sshhhed her again and reached out a hand to stroke her hair back from her forehead. She was quaking and drenched with perspiration. I saw that her wrists were handcuffed and fastened behind her to a sturdy chair. I nodded at Cate and asked softly, "Is she okay?"

"Uh huh," Darnelle murmured. "She's been delirious, but I think she's alright. Ms. Fury—"

"Nell. And keep it down."

"—Nell." Darnelle Comey commenced to weep noiselessly. I held her for a minute while I glanced up at the room's windows. Both of them appeared to have screens, but if we could pull them off without making a commotion we were close enough to ground level to simply hop out.

I tried to get Darnelle to calm down. I noticed Cate Jones was bound, too, though not to any piece of furniture. I had a small jackknife attached to my keychain—it might take a few minutes but I thought I could slice through the rope.

"Darnelle...hey!"

"What?!" Darnelle jerked around frantically, expecting the worst.

"Sshhh, sorry. Listen." I fumbled in another of my pockets. "Were you at Club Femmes recently?"

162

She thrust her head at me like a startled bird. "Yes! How'd you know? They caught me trespassing there. I walked in on them while—"

She cut herself off midstream when she saw the little silver key clasped between my thumb and forefinger.

I grinned. "Scoot over, will ya?"

I really flummoxed her this time. "How did you get that?" she screeched.

"Keep it low, Darnelle, Jesus." I reached around and fitted the key into the handcuffs. They fell open. "When did they nab you?"

"Yesterday. Umm, late afternoon. I got into Club Femmes through a back window and found that red-haired woman guarding Cate. Wow, I'm so sore..." Darnelle rubbed her fingers over the chafed skin on her wrists.

"What kind of weapon did she have?" I was about to drop the cuffs and key to the floor, then thought better of it. You never know when you'll want a pair of these. I deposited the set into my back pocket and flashed a little private smile.

Darnelle said: "I don't know—I didn't see a gun or anything. Cate was all tied up. I tried to get away and then that other lady arrived. *She* had a gun."

"They cuffed you right there?" I opened the biggest blade on my knife and began hacking at the rope that was binding Cate's ankles. She didn't stir; I feared she was unconscious.

"No," Darnelle replied. "They just kept the gun on me. They put us in a car and drove us straight here. Then they handcuffed me to this chair. It's been almost twenty-four hours."

"Hmm. Well, somebody dropped the key back at Club Femmes." Shit. Progress was slow with the damn knife.

"Oh god, what's going on?" Darnelle unfolded herself from the floor and ran ten fingers through her dark mop of hair.

"Later. Listen, try to rouse her, okay? *Quietly.*"

"Yeah."

I kept sawing while Darnelle Comey knelt and gave Cate's head a gentle shake. I realized the poor kid was stiff, urine-soaked, terrified. And who knows what was wrong with Cate. I asked: "Did they give you water?"

"Uh huh. A couple of times. But no food."

I dug into the rope even harder. I knew we were running out of time. I felt the strand break free. As I was untangling the rope from around Cate's legs, she let out a strangled moan. It sounded as loud as a foghorn in the hushed house.

"Fuck!" I said.

Darnelle clamped a hand over Cate's mouth. Probably not the wisest move psychologically, but the best idea under the circumstances. I pulled Cate to a sitting position. I hissed, "Cate, we're going to help you now. We're going to go through the window and head for my car. As fast as we can, okay?"

Cate Jones had dark liquid eyes just like her sister's. In the subdued glow of my penlight, I could see her staring at me from within a hollow fog of incomprehension. Her skin was chalky, her lips cracked at the corners, the fleshy parts bloodless and raw. I took hold of her hands which were still tied in front of her with rope.

"Cate, I know you're scared but we have to leave now. Can you walk?" I didn't wait for an answer but started hoisting her to her feet. Darnelle helped from the other side. Suddenly footsteps resounded from the far quarters of the house. Somebody turned on a faucet.

I told Darnelle to support Cate, then raced over to the nearest window. It shrieked as I slid it up the jamb. I felt panicked and rammed out the aluminum-framed screen with one hearty kick. As I scurried back to assist Darnelle, a sharp voice cried out from the kitchen. More footsteps, pounding this time. They were onto us.

Darnelle and I tripped headlong out the window, pulling Cate with us. We landed in the vicinity of the topiary gardens and I was on my feet, scrambling to help the others up. Darnelle was surprisingly agile, considering her recent predicament. She and I tugged Cate Jones across the manicured lawn where she'd probably played croquet at some earlier, more unsullied time. Tonight it was all gloom and jeopardy at the old childhood home.

As we reached the roadway, Nadine Flack Novacek let fly a bloodcurdling epithet through the open window. I didn't look back, but I heard a thud as she came out of the house and I knew she was hot on our heels.

27

It was completely dark by now. The rental car huddled up ahead in the shadows of a streetlight. When we got to it I had trouble holding the key steady to get us inside. Nadine was calling out "Stop!" in a steely voice. Gillian Finer must have been trailing us, too; I heard another set of footfalls. Finally I wrenched open the tinny door. Darnelle and I piled Cate into the back seat and slipped into the buckets, jamming down the locks.

As I fumbled with the ignition, I heard a loud crack against the driver's seat window. Nadine was leering through the glass, her fist coiled around a hunk of pistol. She rapped the barrel against the car and pulled fruitlessly at the door handle.

I guess she was afraid to fire in this relatively inhabited neighborhood. Her mistake. I gunned the accelerator and the Toyota shot forward. It fishtailed a little, knocking Nadine to the ground. In the slit of rearview mirror I saw Gillian help her up. They were in the Camaro in no time, the sound of its engine causing even more racket to reverberate down the street.

"Look out!" Darnelle screamed.

I caught my breath and swerved right, barely missing a pipsqueak kid on a banana bike who was meandering down the center of the road. I felt the car skidding in an unstoppable 180 degree arc. The child scampered out of the way, but the Camaro was upon us. I saw Gillian Finer flinch as their right fender rammed into the Toyota along our right rear side. The Camarro stalled. We were still rolling, though, and I swiveled my head manically to see if everyone was okay. "Go!" Darnelle croaked, and I pointed us back down the road that led out of the canyon.

"What's happening back there?" I asked tersely, reaching up a hand to wipe my brow. The sweat was making my eyes sting.

Darnelle cursed. "They got the car started."

"Shit." I upped the pressure on the gas pedal. We flew down the curving road; thankfully, few other cars were a-round. I wondered if anybody besides the kid had witnessed our collision. I tried to concentrate on the mission at hand. I felt disadvantaged that I didn't know the streets in the area. Then I realized Nadine probably didn't either.

Cate Jones was whimpering in the back seat. Darnelle was breathing rapidly, but otherwise maintaining her cool. I launched into a little pep talk: we were almost to the open road, we'd be out of danger soon, we were going to be fine. God, I could be such a phony sometimes.

Darnelle said: "They're right behind us, Nell."

I bore down on the accelerator and felt the car lift off the ground as we passed over a bump. A vehicle coming toward us peeled onto the opposite shoulder and blasted a few shrill honks. I slowed a little, then picked up the pace again when the specter of the white automobile filled up the rearview mirror.

We were almost to the turn-off for the Pacific Coast Highway. I maneuvered a few more corners and saw the swell of muddy-colored ocean through the windshield. I merged onto the highway heading northwest. I cranked my head for an instant and thought I saw Finer training the gun out the window of the Camaro's passenger side.

I don't know how long we traveled that way, raising havoc with our lives and terrorizing a slew of other drivers. I also don't know if Finer or Novacek ever fired a gunshot; if they did, they failed to hit the Toyota. Suddenly a cacophony of sirens rose up over the sound of the engine. I felt immense relief and let myself slow to sixty-five. Nadine had a different reaction. I heard her downshift violently, then she whirred across the center lane and tried to pass us. Darnelle screamed. A slat-sided pickup truck was bearing straight down on the Camaro.

Nadine Flack Novacek jerked her vehicle hard to the left. The pickup never wavered. I tried to maintain control of my own car while I watched, horrified, as the Camaro tumbled down a short, steep bank, flipped a few times, and crashed to a halt against an outcropping of craggy rocks.

The next couple of hours were an emotional and logistical nightmare. I managed to steer the car onto a sandy side road and lurch to a stop. Then I promptly stumbled out and vomited all over the base of a sign for Topanga State Beach. Darnelle, meanwhile, was rooted in her seat. Cate Jones seemed to be conked out again in the rear. I asked Darnelle to stay and watch Cate, then I jogged back along the highway until I got to the scene of the accident.

A phalanx of emergency and law enforcement vehicles was already clogging the area. Rubber-neckers were slowing up traffic on the Pacific Coast Highway and witnesses were babbling out their stories to no one in particular. The whole scenario exhausted me.

I forced myself to buck up and take a careful look at what was going on. Through the technicolor blur of red and blue flashing lights, I noted members of the California Highway Patrol, the Los Angeles County Sheriff's Department, the local cops, and the state park police. Paramedics were clustered near the overturned car, and I thought I saw some dude in a park ranger hat rush by with a stretcher.

This would be a jurisdictional mess, alright. Just wait till the boys from homicide and organized crime got into the thick of it. I didn't want to have anything to do with sorting it all out, but I knew I better talk to somebody fast. I approached a beat cop and introduced myself as the driver of the other speeding automobile.

She plopped me into the front seat of her squad car and listened to my side of the story. She turned out to be a handy liaison for the rest of the night. She told me somebody had witnessed our little crash on Toyopa Drive and called the authorities. That's why so many sirens had converged at once. She also said the driver of the Camaro was presumed dead— they were waiting on official notification. The other woman had been thrown from the car and, though battered, would probably make it.

I told her my two companions in the Toyota up the road might need medical attention. She squawked something into her radio, then took me around to speak with some of the other honchos.

The semi-automatic handgun that Novacek and Finer had brandished had landed under a tumbleweed not far from Gillian's body. That helped verify my account of a high-speed dash for our lives. I gave a brief rundown of my rescue of Darnelle and Cate, and suggested they call Inspector Peter Little of the S.F.P.D. for further information on how this all connected to a series of deaths in San Francisco. One disgruntled uniform growled at me with pure venom, but everybody else seemed to think I was square. After reaching Little at home, they told me I could go—as long as I swore to give a lengthy statement tomorrow and contact the law up north, too, as soon as I returned to San Francisco.

It was after 10 p.m. I decided to leave the Toyota overnight, and went in search of the woman in blue to beg a ride to the hospital. I wanted to find out how Darnelle Comey and Cate Jones were faring. Besides, I had no place else to go. It was then I noticed a small silver-haired person traversing in my direction across a rocky stretch of ground. I'll be damned—Martha of Toyopa Drive. Turns out she was the one who'd called the cops. And after a glimpse of the ten o'clock news, she'd driven down to the beach to see for herself what was going on.

I was a little embarrassed explaining my subterfuge to Martha, whose last name I finally learned—Coakley. She didn't seem to mind, though. She was happy to have me on hand to pump me for information. She also agreed to take me to the hospital. I was told Cate was weakened, dehydrated, and suffering from shock. They wanted to observe her for a few days at the Santa Monica facility. Darnelle had been treated and released. I found her in a women's room off one of the waiting areas, morosely trying to sponge herself clean.

She greeted me with a big, rangy hug when I walked into the garishly lit lavatory. "Nell!"

I smiled at her. "Hi, Darnelle."

"Wow." She shook her head, her wet braid flopping around and dampening my cheek. "Is it always like this?"

"What?"

"Private investigating."

"Naw. Sometimes it's really exciting."

"But..." God, she could be so gullible.

"I'm just kidding, sweetie," I said. I steered her toward the exit. "The cops will want to talk to you tomorrow morning."

"I still don't understand what happened...how you found us..."

"I'll explain it later. I've got a place for us to stay tonight."

She sighed. "Thanks, Nell."

"Let's go."

28

Martha Coakley had offered us her spare bedroom for the night. I was loathe to return to that neighborhood, but I realized I was only being superstitious. I'd told the police about the threat to burn down the Jones' house. When we rolled past, an unmarked sedan with "cop" written all over it was positioned in view of the sculpture garden lawn. It was probably an unnecessary precaution—there were no bodies to incinerate, after all—but I didn't mind the extra effort on the part of our public servants.

Darnelle Comey went to take a shower while I settled down with Martha at the kitchen table. She produced three juice glasses with painted orange sunbursts chipping off from the sides and a fifth of Wild Turkey. It wasn't my poison of choice, but it would do in a pinch.

Fifteen minutes later, Darnelle emerged from the bathroom and took a place at the table. My turn for the shower. Martha had laid out sweatsuits for us to change into. Mine was a turquoise velour number that bunched around the ankles and was unpleasantly tight across the middle. What the hell. Darnelle looked pretty silly, too, in her kelly green set with a palm tree applique across the chest. I heard the two of them tittering happily as I walked back to the kitchen.

"Ha ha ha," Martha crooned. "I just love your friend, Nell. She's going to be your assistant, eh?"

Darnelle looked mortified. She slugged back some whiskey and said, "Oh...no. I'm still in school. I meant maybe, you know, afterwards..."

I chuckled humorlessly and took a tiny swallow from my glass. I was beat. We spent another half hour getting acquainted, then I told them I was hitting the sack. Darnelle hopped up and padded after me as we said our good nights to Martha.

She had put us in what looked like an old kids' room. There was a clutter of sports memorabilia on all the surfaces and a narrow pair of bunk beds covered in brown plaid spreads. I hoisted myself onto the top. Those bottom bunks made me paranoid. Darnelle didn't seem to mind; she slid right into the lower level. I told Darnelle what had been going on as we lay in our parallel slots in the darkened room. When I said I knew it was Jed Flack who hired E-Z, she claimed to know nothing further about his motivation. She'd gone to Club Femmes because her boss told her to keep probing there.

Darnelle said: "You found Cate Jones. So you solved the case!"

I stretched my arms high over my head, then decided to pull off the constricting sweatshirt. Whew, much better. "Yeah. But there're some loose ends."

"What's going to happen to Olive Jones?"

"That's one of them."

"Nell?"

"Hmmm?"

"Will you put in a good word for me with my boss?"

I swear. Every time this woman pissed me off, she made me laugh afterwards. "Ummm—if I do, will you let me keep your pick locks?"

"I wondered what happened to those!"

She knocked off moments later, letting out a scratchy rhythmic snore. I couldn't seem to fall asleep, despite my exhaustion. Images kept flashing through my mind of the tumbling Camaro, Olive Jones when I first saw her at the bar,

Olive Jones waving a handgun, Cate frozen in a frightened stupor, and a pair of brilliant red fish dancing in perfect synch across a bowl of dazzlingly clear water.

The following morning, Darnelle put her sweatsuit back on. I couldn't bear the thought and opted for my crusty but comfortable Levis-and-Loveless outfit. It made me think of Rae in the fondest of ways. Then I called a cab to take us to the entrance to Topanga State Beach. The damn Toyota had been towed. Or stolen. I fumed a little over the loss of my cassettes, then asked the cabbie to take us to the nearest office of the car rental agency. He dumped us on a main drag in Santa Monica and I went in to plead my case.

After a couple of phone calls, the harassed clerk determined the car had in fact been towed. She said the company would retrieve it as long as I paid the towing fees. I decided good riddance and coughed up some more of Olive Jones' money. So much for that hunk of dough, I thought, mentally tallying the cost of a couple of plane tickets and other miscellanea. I shrugged and slipped the clerk another twenty for her trouble.

Darnelle and I found a nearby cafe and downed generous portions of huevos rancheros. She seemed to be recovering well from her ordeal—she was perky as all get out. In fact, she was driving me nuts. We caught another taxi to the police station and gave our statements. Then I handed Darnelle some cash to get to the airport and catch a flight north.

"See ya," I said.

"Nell..."

"Yeah, yeah." I suffered another of her sloppy hugs. "You take care, Darnelle."

I wandered down the broad white sidewalk giving myself a little time to unwind. It took me a minute to remember what day it was—oh yeah, Monday. I popped some change into a paper box and sat on the curb reading the *L.A. Times*. There was more bad news about Feinstein, the Cubs, and the turmoil surrounding the International AIDS Conference. Then I found a small item about Nadine's death buried in the Metro section. The article said she may have been involved in a Bay

Area murder scheme, but there was no mention of Joe Lockenwood. Hmm... I had told the cops he was one of the masterminds behind the plot to kidnap and kill the Joneses. I wondered what they'd do with the information.

Finally I felt ready to visit Cate Jones. I found her sitting up in a hospital bed with a copy of *Lesbian Connection* propped open on her knees. Either she'd had visitors already, or she'd done some quick work on the hospital staff. I smiled. Cate looked freshly scrubbed, her fine brown hair falling in a shiny curtain around her shoulders. Her skin was wan, though, and a pair of purplish rings gave her eyes a haunted cast. I approached her slowly.

"I see you got some reading material."

She flinched and crushed the pages of the magazine together.

"Cate," I said softly, "I'm sorry. Do you remember who I am?"

She nodded uncertainly.

"My name's Nell Fury. I helped you get away last night. And—" I paused. "—your sister hired me about a week ago to find you. I'm a private investigator."

"Olive did? What is...is she okay?"

"Well..." I had no idea how much Cate knew. I asked, "Have you talked to the police?"

"Yeah."

"So you know that Nadine died last night?"

"Um-hm. And Gillian..." Cate's voice caught. "I was so in love with her."

I said quietly, "She's going to make it."

Tears welled up in the edges of Cate's eyes. She didn't say anything, so I sat in a visitor's chair and asked her to tell me what had happened.

It was pretty much what I thought. Gillian Finer had met Cate at a bar, courted her, and encouraged her to work as a dancer at Club Femmes.

"I fell for her," Cate explained. "I just wanted to be with her all the time. I didn't *need* the job, I just..." She started crying. "I just wanted to be in her world, you know? I...I just wanted her so much."

Cate said that after being together almost a year, Gillian had convinced her to change her will—she'd argued something about recognizing lesbian relationships. Then one day a couple of weeks ago, Gillian, Godfrey Bellinski, and a woman she'd never met before—Nadine—had kidnapped her and sequestered her away in the Orinda house. From their conversations, Cate figured out they planned to murder both her and her sister.

"So they sent that note that got Olive to come to San Francisco to try to find you?"

"Yes." Cate was clutching her arms through the gauzy cotton of the hospital robe.

I thought for a second. "Did you really live in that flat off 17th Street?"

"Yes," Cate repeated. "They were going to try to trap Olive there."

"God, it's so awful."

The tears were still sliding down Cate's cheeks. "Nell, the police wouldn't tell me anything about Olive."

"Ohhh...she's alright." I sighed. "Except she's been arrested. For murdering Bellinski. And for shooting that other guy, too, the man mixed up in—"

"But *they're* the murderers! She was trying to save me. How can—"

"I know, Cate. We might be able to argue that the killing was justifiable."

She sniffled, "I need to see her."

I asked her how long the doctors wanted her to stay in the hospital. Cate said she didn't know, they wouldn't talk to her. Then I asked if she knew where she'd go when she got out. She just shrugged, looking baffled by all the upheaval in her life. I wanted to know just one more thing—if Cate knew what Gillian and her cohorts were planning to do with the Jones' money.

She dropped her chin. "Bellinski was selling the club. They got a tip that there was all this money to be made in the prostitution business in Nevada. Casinos, too. And in San Francisco, upscale hotels." Cate's voice dripped with disdain. "But they *needed* more money to make money. It's so sick."

It sounded like plain old capitalism to me. But I didn't say anything.

"And you know what else," Cate went on, raising her head so I could see the defiant glint in her ravaged eyes. "I think Gillian was faking it all along. I think Bellinski set her up to seduce me. He already knew Olive and me...knew we were wealthy. I think they planned the whole goddamn thing from the minute Bellinski heard I moved to San Francisco."

I was glad to hear her so riled up. Nothing like being lethally double-crossed to bring out a healthy dose of rage. "Cate," I said, "did they ever mention the name Flack?"

She frowned. "You mean Jed Flack?"

"Uh huh."

"I think he was a friend of Bellinski's, but..." She shrugged.

"So he wasn't part of the kidnapping scheme?"

She looked startled. "I...I don't know."

"Nevermind." I smiled, pointing at the *Lesbian Connection* that lay crinkled on the bedsheet. "The nurses bring you that?"

I heard Cate Jones laugh for the first time. "No, some old friends of mine stopped by this morning."

"That's a good issue. I liked the section about whether or not vegetarian s/m dykes should wear real leather."

Cate gawked. I could see a whole new appreciation light up in her eyes as she drank me in from head to toe.

"You're—"

"We are everywhere," I mugged, and went to grant her a goodbye kiss on the cheek. I gave her a business card and told her to be in touch when she got back to the City. She forgot to thank me for saving her life, but then there's only so much recognition you can expect in a fly-by-night profession like this one.

29

My plane taxied into the San Francisco airport at 2:18 p.m. Everything looked beautiful through the yellowed postage stamp window—I felt like I'd been gone for ages. Since I hadn't been able to reach Phoebe on the telephone, I cruised the line of waiting cabs on the off chance of finding her. No luck. So I hopped a maddeningly slow shuttle bus that oozed its way north and dead-ended at the Transbay Terminal south of Market.

As Darnelle had said, I solved my case, so why didn't I feel more buoyant? I kicked at a flyaway bit of newspaper and considered going immediately to my office to start salvaging my business affairs. Then I remembered the busted door and wondered if Mary had had it fixed. I'd have to dish out some more of my dwindling cash supply to reimburse her.

I changed my mind and decided to hightail it home to feed Flannery and Carson. Then I changed it again when I remembered my vow to check in with Inspector Little. Might as well get that over with. So I weaved through the early rush hour crunch of pedestrians, crossed Market Street, and entered the building that housed the Continent West Detective

Agency. I wanted to bring Tad Greenblatt along to sort of smooth over my encounter with old Peanut.

I found Tad and his colleagues in the middle of a raucous birthday party. A wad of chocolate frosting hung from Tad's upper lip and a plastic cup of fuzzy gold liquid rested in his catcher's mitt of a hand.

I laughed and said to the group, "Investigating your endless capacity for indolence, I see."

"Get a load of who's talking," Tad retorted. Then he set down his cup and threw a massive arm across my shoulders. "Nellie, you son of a gun."

Everybody got into the action and before long I was tipping champagne and relating the details of Cate Jones' rescue. They had all heard about the saga. Turns out Gillian Finer had foolishly tried to save her hide by spilling the beans to the police. She'd hoped to pin all the blame on Bellinski and Nadine Novacek.

The resulting furor was bigger news up here than it had been in Los Angeles. COYOTE had come forward and condemned the late Godfrey Bellinski and other entrepreneurs who habitually wrested control of the sex industry away from women. One of the gay rights organizations had held a press conference to explain that, even if some individuals abused domestic partnership agreements, the concept remained crucial for ensuring the validity of lesbian and gay relationships. And a legal support network for Olive Jones was in the formative stages. Gosh, what a town.

But I'd be showing my supportive stripes, too. I'd already decided to be a witness in Olive's defense if the need arose.

Tad Greenblatt gave me a little grief when I finally pulled him away from the office. In fact, he kept it up all the way to the cop shop. Proud as he secretly was of me, he also—not so secretly—objected to my tendency to recklessly endanger myself. What the heck, I was starting to feel pretty good. Then Little used me for a verbal punching bag, but that didn't bother me either. By the time I made it back to Ramona Avenue, I was wondering who would play the part of me in the sure to be upcoming movie version of *Nell Fury, Private Eye.*

Naturally, these bursts of ego come and go, rare and fleeting as a warm summer's day in San Francisco. I fed the fish—who looked none the worse for my absence—and got out the makings of a tomato sandwich. While slathering it together, I started obsessing on Joe Lockenwood and Jed Flack. Neither fellow had as yet been scathed by their probable involvement in murder and mayhem. Except for Bellinski and Held, it was women who were paying the price so far. Hmm.

I chomped down my supper while taking a quick stock of my mail and phone messages. Reporters made up a bulk of the latter—I jotted down the numbers and would deal with some of them tomorrow. Including Lydia Luchetti, who was hot to pen another "Women and Crime" exposé.

I pulled off my grimy outfit and found the Pebble Beach sweatshirt clumped on the bathroom floor. I slipped it on and gazed out the window for a while. Then I stretched out on the bed and balanced the phone on my stomach. I pressed seven digits.

A familiar rasp said, "Hello?" after only one ring.

"Hi, Willy. It's Nell Fury."

He didn't say anything, but I heard a match strike in the background and a long intake of breath.

"Willy, I'm sorry about Nadine's death."

Still no response. That made sense: he probably didn't care about his wife's death and, besides, I was indirectly responsible for her car crash. What could Willy Novacek say? I changed the subject. "Can I talk to Jed, please?"

"He can't come to the phone."

"Willy, Willy, Willy." I paused, the tune to "Louie, Louie" suddenly congealing itself in my brain. "Willy, it's me, Nell, remember our conversation the other night?"

He snapped at me. "I remember who you are! But Jed's not...available right now—"

I started to speak, but he continued, "And don't come over here—we won't let you in!"

"Okay." I didn't know whether to play it stern or consoling. I tried a bit of both. "But I'm not going to drop this. A lot of people's lives got fucked up because of something Jed's involved with. He's in the public eye, Willy—you can't keep covering for him forever."

"I knooow, Nell." I must have struck a nerve. Willy lowered his voice and added, "I don't know what to do."

"Do you know anymore about what's going on with him?"

"No."

I waited. I listened to him breathe for a while, then said, "Talk to me, Willy."

He groaned, "Okay, look, we're having an argument about Boom Properties. Jed thinks we should keep our hand in the hotel plans. But I don't want to have anything to do with a project like that. Besides, Jed will be in trouble when the press gets wind of it."

"Ummm."

"Nell, I know what you're thinking, but he hasn't done anything *illegal*."

"Ummm."

Willy was getting mad again. "What do you want? What's going to make you believe that?"

"I need to talk to him, Willy."

I heard the receiver drop with a forceful clunk on the other end of the line. I lay there flexing my ankles and working out other kinks in my sore muscles. Last time I'd inspected my left shoulder, the wound from the grazing bullet looked rather artful; I thought I'd end up with a tiny lightning bolt scar. I was staring at the hill of laundry on my closet floor when Willy came back on the line.

"Listen, Nell." He was back to his old warm self. "Jed's in the bathtub right now, but he says he'll talk with you tomorrow."

"Great."

"He says he'll meet you at Golden Gate Fields."

"What?"

"Before the start of the third race, in front of the viewing ring."

"What is this? Are we in the middle of a John Le Carré novel?"

Willy made a throaty noise that might have been a laugh. "He doesn't want to be seen with you anyplace, umm, you know."

"I *don't* know, but what the hell."

"Thanks, Nell. You're nice."

"I am not nice."

"Well. I like you."

"See ya, Willy."

"Bye."

"Bye."

I spent the next couple of hours at the laundromat. I killed the time reading back issues of *Camera Obscura* that I'd never been able to finish. The feminist film journal couldn't have had a more appropriate name. Finally, I trudged home with my arms full of clean clothes in brown paper bags. Then I changed into my favorite black jeans and a soft white T-shirt and called Tammie Rae Tinkers.

She agreed to meet me at Amelia's. When I walked in half an hour later, nervous flutter at the base of my ribcage, I found her and Phoebe bellied up to the bar in conversation with a Tina Turner-lookalike bartender. They all gave me kisses, Tina included. Then I ordered a martini—the last one had been so tasty that I wanted to try another under less onerous circumstances. This one was just as delicious.

"Good to see you," Rae said. We moved to a table on the raised platform that runs along one side of the bar. It makes for a perfect view of all the women as they enter Amelia's. Rae was staring only at me, though, and Phoebe was leaning back in her chair, eyeing us with total amusement.

"Yeah, Nell," Phoebe said, grinning. "Aren't you a caution."

I repeated my tale of adventure in Pacific Palisades, and the three of us passed an amiable Monday evening discussing crime and punishment, the tactics of Earth First!, Phoebe's budding romance with Johnnie Blue, and whether or not I should buy a new car. Nothing was decided, except that Rae would spend the night with me. When we left, Phoebe was still chuckling over the sight of the smitten lovebirds. Ha. Wait till I got together with her and Johnnie—I could match her tease for tease.

Rae made a big fuss over Flannery and Carson. Judging from the way their sleek fins flapped rapidly in the water when she tapped the side of the bowl, they appreciated such an eager show of devotion. But I focused all my attention on Rae that night. Several hours later, I was stroking the rise of her hip and biting sleepily at her neck when she interrupted me with a question.

"So is it all over? Your case with the Jones twins?"

"Ummm." I sighed. "It's funny, Rae, I suppose it *is* over, but once you start digging around in the world of commerce and power-broking, you uncover all this greed, all this corruption, and it's like...you've just scratched the surface. It's over. But it'll never be over."

I could see her teeth glinting in the dark. "So is that why you're a private eye? To stamp out corruption everywhere? Like a modern-day Wonder Woman?"

"God, are you kidding? A two-bit player like me? Only in my dreams." I laughed. "Besides, sodomy is still illegal in about half the states. I'm a bit of a lawbreaker myself."

"Oh yeah? Show me."

Some time after that, Rae rolled onto her back and eased up a sheet. She asked quietly, "So what are you going to do now, Nell?"

I sighed, then brushed her cheek with the back of my knuckles. "I guess I'll just keep scratching the surface."

30

I took BART to Golden Gate Fields late the next morning. The day had dawned coolish and damp. I wore my olive green trenchcoat buttoned up to the neck, but I wished I'd put another layer on underneath. I fell into step with all the other drably attired racetrackers, and handed over the price of admission. I wouldn't have been surprised to see Bogie emerge from the fog that hung in opaque gray chunks under the eaves of the main building.

I was a little too distracted to concentrate on the ponies, but I bought a program anyway and gave it a quick read-through. A gelding named Stop 'N Go looked promising in the first. I placed a cautious bet and huddled in the upper bleachers watching Stop 'N Go perform accordingly. I decided to bag the pari-mutuel pool for now and went to hunt down a root beer. They only sold Pepsi and Sprite. This wasn't shaping up to be my day.

I leaned against a support post, hands thrust deep in my coat pockets, and watched all the mini-melodramas unfold around me. A mother-daughter team right beside me bickered over whether to drop ten or twenty on their favorite in the next race. An old man with a cigar molded to his drooping lower lip was scooping up discarded betting slips in hopes of finding a winning ticket abandoned by mistake. And a blind guy in a natty bow tie was nudging a friend for the latest odds on the ever-changing stats board.

But I didn't see City Supervisor Jed Flack among the crowd. Oh well, maybe he wasn't the punctual sort.

At five minutes before the start of the third, I made my way over to the viewing ring. There he was, wearing the same stone-washed jacket I'd seen him in last time. He hadn't noticed my approach, so I took a minute to check him out thoroughly. Graying temples, slightly orangy tan, a well-placed dimple that gave character to his otherwise flaccid chin. Underneath the jacket he wore a pale yellow polo shirt tucked into high-waisted brown corduroys. He looked like somebody trying overly hard to dress casually.

He jumped when I came up behind him.

I said: "So here we are, Mr. Flack. Was all this secrecy necessary?"

"Ms. Fury." His smile was stretched as tight as a painter's canvas. "I was planning to come here today anyway. I...I feel anonymous here."

I shrugged.

"Would you like a drink?" Flack asked.

"No, I want to watch the race."

I didn't really; I was just being obstinate. We shuffled outside to the deck and stood silently while the horses got settled in the starting gates. I waited for the gun to sound before asking Flack why he'd been at the track with Gillian Finer.

He raised his voice to be heard over the cheering crowd. A few of his neck veins popped out like ropy twigs. "She was a friend of Godfrey Bellinski's. He thought the two of us should get acquainted."

"So you'd be closer pals throughout the kidnapping."

"No!" The race was nose to nose coming down the backstretch. Flack ignored it, a small pitiful plea in his tone as he pivoted to look at me straight on. "Ms. Fury, you have to believe me, I didn't know anything about the murder plot! They—Godfrey and Nadine—they told me they had the necessary capital. They just needed me to, you know, introduce them to people in Nevada, find property..." His voice trailed off.

"That's what you were doing in Nye County, right? Milking your connections, scouting property—"

"Yes." Flack's dimple bobbed. "But I'm giving it up now. I...it just doesn't look good after what's happened."

"That's an understatement." A jockey in green silks came sailing over the finish line, butt raised high as he slowed his winning horse. A mix of groans and yelps rose up from the stands.

Flack jerked his head, startled by the sudden commotion.

I said: "So you're telling me you were mixed up with Bellinski, Finer, and your ex-wife Nadine, and you never knew they intended to murder the Jones twins?"

"That's right. But I did get concerned because they started acting...oh, a little strangely. That's why I hired a firm to see what *you* were up to. Doesn't that prove my innocence?"

I didn't respond.

"You have to understand," Flack said, shivering. "Nadine was very persuasive. She and Willy and I had worked out an arrangement that, uh, benefited us all. When she presented me with new ideas, it was hard to turn her down."

"Like, say, for an investment option in Boom Properties. Hidden under her name."

His head bobbed up and down. "I haven't done anything outside the law, Ms. Fury. That's why I agreed to see you. To convince you of that."

"Oh great!" I stomped my foot and felt a bit of hot dog squish under my toe. "There's the law, sure, and then there's your own personal sense of integrity. You're supposed to be pro-tenant and pro-working stiff. And here you are, engaging in shady, misogynist business ventures and planning to reap a profit by decimating affordable housing and wiping out jobs. And that's not to mention staying firmly rooted in the closet. Hmmph!"

Flack focused his eyes way off across the misty track, spine held ramrod stiff.

"You know what?" I continued. "I believe you. I don't think you were in on the murder plot. But that doesn't make a whole lot of difference. You're still a fucking hypocrite."

Jed Flack turned to face me again, his tiny frown reflecting more sadness than anger. Perhaps he agreed with my character assessment. I crossed my arms over my chest and turned back toward the building.

We were walking inside when he said, "Ms. Fury, it's not as simple as it used to be. When I first moved to California, I was full of ideals. I wanted to be everything my father wasn't. A crusader for justice, a politician who really cared. Now I'm a middle-aged man and I'm tired. I want my privacy back. I want a little security." His face split one more time into a melancholy frown. "I'm turning out just like my father."

"What'll you do if this all comes out in the press? About the whorehouse? And Boom Properties?"

"Ohhhh." He sighed. "I used to be more worried about things like that. Now I'm not so sure it'd really hurt me. What am I, anyway, but a guy who's trying to make a buck?"

I let that sit for a moment. Then I asked, "Do you know Joe Lockenwood?"

Flack said no. But he admitted he knew that Lockenwood and Bellinski had been tight. He also fed me another bit of information that cleared up part of the puzzle. According to Flack, Lockenwood had powerful friends on both the L.A. and San Francisco police forces. They'd probably been hoping for some stepped up kickbacks from Lockenwood's most recent schemes. No wonder some elements of the S.F.P.D. had seemed satisfied to let Olive Jones take the fall.

"How can you stand it?" I asked Flack.

"I'm not sure I can, Ms. Fury. I'm only telling you how it works." Flack wheezed out a long breath. Then he buttoned his jacket, squared his shoulders in that trust-me-I'm-a-civil-servant way, and headed out toward the nearest exit.

31

It really was all over now, or so I thought. Two days later, I was back at the office listening to my decade-old Au Pairs tape and trying to get a handle on things. That involved drinking endless cups of joe, chewing an occasional Fig Newton, and trying to make baskets into the trash can with the useless junk I was laboriously cleaning out of my desk. I wondered if poets got their inspiration this way—I'd have to ask Pinky.

I'd spent part of yesterday building a makeshift partition in my apartment. I wanted Pinky to have a room of her own when she arrived for the summer. I don't think you'd call my place a two-bedroom now, but it was functional. I'd spruced it up a bit, and bought Pinky a futon and other necessities like towels and sheets. All of that—along with the cost of repairing the warehouse door, and the inevitable May rent—had just about depleted my funds. So much for a new car or, for that matter, repairing the Rabbit. Oh well. I'd have to go back to relying on the Schwinn. I was overdue for a long, sweaty two-wheeled workout anyway.

I'd also caught up with Lydia Luchetti yesterday. She was all fired up about her "Women and Crime" article for *Re-View*, which she planned to write as soon as she finished the piece on COYOTE. Plus, she was determined to drag Jed Flack's name through the mud. So was another reporter—a fellow from the *San Francisco Bay Times* who'd tracked me down early this morning. I didn't begrudge them their efforts. I was just having a momentary lapse of faith in the power of the press. That is, as it affects those with even more power. We'll see.

I sunk a particularly impressive bank shot and was fantasizing about getting drafted by the Chicago Bulls when I heard the clip-clip-clip of approaching footsteps. I planted my oxfords flat to the floor and awaited what I hoped would be a flesh-and-blood client. Instead, a coat hanger of a guy in a baggy postal service uniform hovered uncertainly at the warehouse entrance and eyed Mary's latest artistic triumphs. I cleared my throat. The postman jumped.

"Who are you looking for?" I called out.

"Nell Fury."

"You found her."

I crossed the cement floor and signed for the certified letter. The return address was unfamiliar to me; I thought the town might be a small beach community in Southern California. I thanked the mail carrier and retreated to my magenta easy chair. The envelope was extremely weighty with a fine silver band rimming the edges. I tore the flap and pulled out a piece of matching stationery. The message was succinct.

> Dear Miss Fury,
>
> My associate Joe Lockenwood requested that I contact you. He admires the finesse and discretion with which you dispatched your recent obligations. He holds no hard feelings about the debacle at the Cliff House. Should you ever seek employment in any of our affiliated operations, Mr. Lockenwood suggests you get in touch with me at the address indicated.
>
> Most sincerely,
> Fingers McGee

Fingers. Give me a break.

I crumpled the note in my left hand and felt the bite of a paper cut zing along the soft flesh at the base of my thumb. Damn. I slam dunked the missive into the trash. Then I had a change of heart. Old Fingers might come in handy sometime.

I plucked out the paper, returned it to its envelope, and carried the offending item over to my file drawer. I was trying to decide between "F" for Fingers, "L" for Lockenwood, and "S" for Scumbag when I heard more footsteps. This time it sounded like clip-clop-clip-clop-clip-clop. I looked up to see a pair of brunette heads outlined in the doorway against the hazy glare of the midday sun.

I gulped. "Olive. Cate."

I stepped forward slowly. Scrutinizing each of them in turn, I thought what a fetching pair they would make under better circumstances. Today they had a wasted look about them, and no wonder. Cate probably just got out of the hospital; and Olive, the slammer.

As if reading my mind Olive said, "I was released on bail yesterday."

"Well, come on in." I gestured back toward my corner office.

"We can't stay," Cate said. She still had raccoon rings around her eyes and a woeful bend in her elegant neck. But there was a confident edge to her voice now. I noticed her hair was shorter than Olive's and her manner a bit more self-possessed. Otherwise they were perfectly matched, right down to their Katharine Hepburn-esque slacks and swingy oversized jackets.

Olive appeared jittery as she had the first night I met her. She said, "We wanted to thank you, Nell. You really came through for us."

Aw, shucks. "I'm glad you're both okay," I responded. Then I flashed on something that had been bugging me. "Olive, you know the handkerchief you, umm, borrowed from my desk? With the brown and white checks?"

"Um-hm..."

"I found it outside Club Femmes. You know anything about that?"

"Oh." She sighed. "It must have fallen out of my pocket. After I...rescued you that day at the Cliff House, I went to the club to look for Cate."

"I was there," Cate stated, infinite hatred seeping through her pinched words. She shook her head sharply. "For part of the time, anyway. They kept moving me around."

Olive threaded her arm through her sister's and let out another sad breath. "I must have just missed you that day."

"Speaking of lost items..." I trotted back to my desk and drew Olive's alligator purse from the drawer that no longer locked. I'd stuck it there today, not knowing what else to do with it. I handed it over.

Olive said: "Oh! I thought the police had that."

"Nope." I smiled, but gave no further explanation.

Olive shook her head. "You know, I reported my credit cards lost and they offered me emergency credit. For the motel room and everything. I guess that's how the cops traced me there." She guffawed. "Pretty stupid of me."

Hmm. I'd forgotten that little detail. I asked Cate if she really left a message at the motel asking her sister to come home. She said no—Gillian or Nadine must have faked it. They knew Olive's whereabouts because Olive had left the name of her motel on the answering machine in Pacific Palisades. Another sloppy move.

Olive was fidgeting again. She said to me, "We've got to take off. We're heading back to L.A. until my trial. Then Cate's going to leave the country for a while. She needs to, uh, get away..."

Cate spoke up. "I'm going to Italy. I want to spend some time in Rome, maybe take a sculpture course." She tried to smile. "Learn the language."

I moved my head up and down, but what I really thought was, wow, just like that, eh?

"...so she won't be needing her car," Olive was explaining. "I know yours is out of commission and, well, Cate and I talked about it and decided we didn't compensate you well enough for all your work—"

"—so we want you to have the car while I'm gone," Cate finished.

"You want me to...what?" I blinked.

Cate grinned, this time without hesitation. "Only if you want it. We'll pay up the insurance. I just thought you could take advantage of it while I'm away. It'll be, I don't know, about a year or two."

"A year or two?!"

"It's just an old gas-guzzler. Come on."

I followed the twins out to the sidewalk. Sitting crookedly at the curb, right behind the Rabbit, was a baby blue vintage Mustang convertible with a black interior. It was streaked with dirt and the seat leather was cracked in places, but, nonetheless, it was a beautiful sight to behold. I couldn't believe this was happening.

"I can't—"

"Yes, you can," Cate said. "You'll be doing me a favor. Otherwise Olive would have to deal with it. She's already got a car."

Cate handed me a set of keys on a souvenir ring from Coit Tower, along with the paperwork for the Mustang. Then she stepped inside to call a taxi. They were off to the airport to catch a southbound flight. When the cabbie arrived, the Jones twins hugged me and said goodbye. I watched them rattle away in a haze of exhaust smoke.

I sat in the driver's seat of the Mustang for a while, running my fingers over the steering wheel and the buttery leather upholstery. Even the cracks felt nice. I adjusted the mirrors, messed around with the stick, and imagined zooming around everybody's favorite city with Pinky in the seat beside me. I substituted Phoebe into the scenario, then Rae, then I even gave Tad Greenblatt a chance. He'd probably make me put the top up, though, so his sports coat wouldn't get wrinkled.

I laughed. I scouted the street to see if any potential clients were approaching. No sirree. China Basin was as deserted as the men's room at a k.d. lang concert. So I hustled inside to grab my sunglasses. It was time to take this pony for a ride.

Photo by Donna Tauscher

Elizabeth Pincus is an ex-private eye who now lives in San Francisco. Her writing has appeared in many publications, including *Gay Community News,* the *San Francisco Bay Times,* the *Boston Phoenix* and the *WomanSleuth* anthology series. Currently she is a film critic for the *SF Weekly* and at work on her second Nell Fury novel. (Editor's Note: "The Solitary Twist" will be published by Spinsters Ink in 1993.)

Spinsters Ink was founded in 1978 to produce vital books for diverse women's communities. In 1986 we merged with Aunt Lute Books to become Spinsters/Aunt Lute. In 1990, the Aunt Lute Foundation became an independent non-profit publishing program. In 1992, Spinsters moved to Minneapolis.

Spinsters Ink is committed to publishing full-length novels and non-fiction works that deal with significant issues in women's lives from a feminist perspective: books that not only name crucial issues in women's lives, but more importantly encourage change and growth; books that help make the best in our lives more possible. We are particularly interested in creative works by lesbians.

Other Titles Available From
Spinsters Ink

All The Muscle You Need, Diana McRae	$8.95
As You Desire, Madeline Moore	$9.95
Being Someone, Ann MacLeod	$9.95
Cancer in Two Voices, Butler & Rosenblum	$12.95
Child of Her People, Anne Cameron	$8.95
Considering Parenthood, Cheri Pies	$12.95
Desert Years, Cynthia Rich	$7.95
Elise, Claire Kensington	$7.95
Final Rest, Mary Morell	$9.95
Final Session, Mary Morell	$9.95
High and Outside, Linnea A. Due	$8.95
The Journey, Anne Cameron	$9.95
The Lesbian Erotic Dance, JoAnn Loulan	$12.95
Lesbian Passion, JoAnn Loulan	$12.95
Lesbian Sex, JoAnn Loulan	$12.95
Lesbians at Midlife, ed. by Sang, Warshow & Smith	$12.95
Life Savings, Linnea Due	$10.95
Look Me in the Eye, 2nd Ed., Macdonald & Rich	$8.95
Love and Memory, Amy Oleson	$9.95
Modern Daughters and the Outlaw West, Melissa Kwasny	$9.95
No Matter What, Mary Saracino	$9.95
The Other Side of Silence, Joan M. Drury	$9.95
The Solitary Twist, Elizabeth Pincus	$9.95
Thirteen Steps, Bonita L. Swan	$8.95
Trees Call for What They Need, Melissa Kwasny	$9.95
The Two-Bit Tango, Elizabeth Pincus	$9.95
Vital Ties, Karen Kringle	$10.95
Why Can't Sharon Kowalski Come Home? Thompson & Andrzejewski	$10.95

Spinsters titles are available at your local booksellers, or by mail order through Spinsters Ink. A free catalogue is available upon request.

Please include $1.50 for the first title ordered, and 50 cents for every title thereafter. Visa and Mastercard accepted.

spinsters ink
p.o. box 300170
minneapolis, mn 55403

Ready *for* Take-Off